THE DAIRY

Georgia is the rebellious eldest daughter of George Wilkins, managing director of the family business, Wilkins' Dairy. Studying for a degree in art, she has become involved with a fellow student, Giles. Following lunch with him and his eccentric artist mother, she ends up moving in with them — but finds it hard adjusting to such a dramatically different lifestyle. Meanwhile, George is struggling with difficulties of his own at the dairy. Can father and daughter both deal with their troubles and find contentment?

CHRISSIE LOVEDAY

THE DAIRY

Complete and Unabridged

LINFORD
Leicester

First published in Great Britain in 2014

First Linford Edition
published 2015

A catalogue record for this book is available
from the British Library.

ISBN 978–1–4448–2480–3

Published by
F. A. Thorpe (Publishing)
Anstey, Leicestershire

1

1955

The clatter of milk crates woke both George and Nicola Wilkins.

'Really, they are getting worse. I'll have words with them later,' said George as he got up and stretched. There was a massive crash and the sound of someone swearing. 'Oh lord. There goes the profits for the week.' He walked over to the window where the hapless milkman was standing looking at a crate with broken bottles lying on the ground. 'That's it,' George stormed. 'He can collect his cards. I'm sick of all this inefficiency.'

'Calm down dear,' said Nicola, his wife. 'I'll go and make some tea.'

'And what will you use for milk?'

She ignored him and went downstairs to put the kettle on. As managing director of Wilkins' Dairy, he took everything so personally. It was as if he'd been singled out for the milkman to make a mess outside their house. She went to open the door and saw the poor milkman trying to sweep up the broken glass. He had a dustpan dripping with milk.

'Sorry, missus,' he stumbled. 'Didn't mean to do it.'

'I'm sure you didn't. I'll get some old rags for you to mop up the milk. Be careful not to cut yourself.'

'Was just putting the extra bottles back and it slipped. Bet the boss is pretty narked.'

'He certainly is. I'll go and get something for you to mop up with.' She went inside, and suddenly he decided to scarper. He knew he'd blown it and would probably be out of a job later in the day. He delivered the milk to the next two houses and then drove back to the depot, where he dumped the float and ran away. He'd lose the week's money, but he didn't care. He could not face the boss's anger.

'Here you are,' said Nicola, coming out of the house with a bundle of old cloths. 'Dammit, where's he gone?' She saw his dustpan lying on the ground and the rest of the broken glass lying around. 'Really,' she sighed. 'He does deserve the sack.' She bent down and began to mop up the mess; shuffling most of it into the dustbin before going inside. 'You have my permission to sack that man. He's gone off and left the mess behind him. Really. Where do you find these characters?'

'Nothing to do with me. I only pay them.'

'Well, don't pay him.'

'Don't worry. I'll sack him right away. Now then, where's my tea? And what's for breakfast?'

'I'll do you an egg. And toast. Are the girls moving yet?'

'Don't know,' he muttered as he sat down with the paper.

'Which do I do first? Wake the girls or make your breakfast?'

'Breakfast. Then wake the girls.'

'There's nothing to stop you from calling upstairs to them.'

'I want to read the headlines.'

Nicola sighed. It was the same every morning. He seemed to think she was there just to make breakfast and do everything else as well. Next time on this earth, she swore she'd come back as a man. She slammed bread into the toaster and dumped an egg into a pan. Typically, it broke and spewed egg white all over. George hadn't noticed, so she cracked it completely and turned it into poached egg instead. She buttered his toast and dumped it down in front of him. Then she went to call their daughters.

'Come on, girls. You'll be late. Breakfast's on the table.' She waited till she heard some sound and went back into the kitchen. George hadn't started his breakfast and was still reading. She put three eggs into the pan for herself and the girls, and sighed.

'What's the matter, dear?' mumbled George.

'Nothing. Just sick of you taking me for granted.'

'Yes dear,' was his response.

'You're not even listening to me, are you?'

'Yes dear. I must phone our stock-broker when I get to work.'

'I think Georgia wants to be a stripper.'

'Yes dear.'

'So you'd agree to that?'

'Yes dear. What?'

'Nothing. Just inquiring about your day. Your breakfast's getting cold. Or, rather, it's already cold.'

'Thank you.' He picked up his knife and fork, and complained that his food was cold. Nicola ignored him.

Once breakfast was over and every-one had gone off to work, college and school, Nicola sat down with a fresh pot of tea. What did she have to look forward to? George had the dairy and the girls were busily engaged in their various activities, whilst she had noth-ing except looking after them and their house. She felt totally fed up.

Mrs Henders would be here soon to clean while she sat around trying to occupy herself. Perhaps she could phone one of the other wives. Maybe they would like to meet up for a coffee later? She went into the hall, picked up the phone and dialled Sophie, who was married to George's brother, Henry. There was no reply. She tried the next brother's wife, Victoria.

'Hallo Victoria,' she said when the phone was picked up. 'It's Nicola.'

'Oh, hallo Nicola. Look, do you mind if I call you back? I have a crisis brewing. Gemma is refusing to go to school. I have to sort her out or she'll miss her exam. Bye.'

Gemma was Victoria's youngest daughter. She'd always been something of a rebel, and now it seemed she was seriously causing trouble. Nicola hadn't realised it was exam time. It must be her O-levels; rather early, but she presumed her mother knew best.

So that was it. Her two sisters-in-law

were both busy. Perhaps she could go shopping. There must be something she wanted. Maybe she could go into Town and look at some of the sales.

Mrs Henders arrived and started her usual chatter.

'I'm going out this morning. Do your usual and then lock up before you leave.'

'Certainly, Mrs Wilkins. You going somewhere nice?'

'Just to look at the sales.'

'I hopes as you find summat good.'

'Thank you. I hope so too.'

★ ★ ★

George drove to the dairy in a benevolent mood. He had quite forgotten about the milkman who had dropped his crate outside their home, and was now set on selling his shares in some obscure company that had done a big deal recently. His shares had rocketed and he decided to sell them while the going was good.

'Morning Michael. Everything all right?' Michael was his youngest brother.

'One of the milk delivery team has left us. He dumped the float in the yard with a load of milk left on it. We've no idea where he'd got to in the round. I think he delivers to you?'

'Oh yes. He dropped a crate. I was going to fire him anyway, but was going to wait till the calls come in. Someone's bound to phone and complain soon. Now, if you'll excuse me, I need to make some calls. Let me know if there's anything else.'

'Right you are. Anything else I should know about?'

'Not that I'm aware of. I have stuff to prepare for the Board meeting next week. I suspect it's going to be a dodgy one; the old man is so unwilling to pass on the crown. Mind you, I think it's the Aunts that give us more problems.'

'Don't they always vote with Father?'

'Precisely. Makes us three against three. I really think it's time we removed them from the voting system — but how on earth we do that, I have yet to discover.'

'Best of luck. I'll go and see who's phoned in to complain about lack of milk. I suppose I'd better take the float out and deliver it myself, once we know where he got up to. Wretched man.'

George went into his office and shut the door. He called his stockbroker and told him to see the shares at best price, then settled down to open his post. Nothing much of interest. He put the bills to one side for their accountant to deal with and summoned his secretary.

'A few letters to reply to. I'm sure you know what to say. Nothing too major.'

'Yes, Mr George. Are these the letters?'

'Indeed. There's someone wanting a job in the offices. Tell them we don't have any vacancies at present and thank them for their interest. Tell them we'll file their details, etcetera, and then throw it in the bin. That's it for now. There'll be more later.' His secretary raised her eyebrows, but said nothing. She was used to her boss by now, and just smiled.

'Do you want coffee?'

'Yes please. And ask Henry to give me a moment, will you? Bring him a coffee too.'

George wanted to discuss ways of removing his Aunts from the board — or, at least, removing their voting rights. They really were such a pain.

The two elderly ladies were there because their brother had founded the dairy many years ago, and they had resolutely stayed in place ever since. The dairy had expanded out of all recognition since those early days. His father had begun it when he'd kept a few cows to feed the milk to his chickens, and then started selling the spare milk to his customers who used to buy the eggs. He'd seen a niche in the market, and rapidly expanded the herd. Since those early days, he'd gradually brought more farms into the business, and had bought several milk tankers to drive round to them. Wilkins' Dairy was born, and they now covered a huge area of London and the Home

10

Counties. Geoffrey Wilkins was a self-made man and knew it — and made sure all his sons remembered it.

He had retired from the actual running of the dairy after his wife had died, about four years ago. His three sons had taken over, having been trained in each department in their youth. He hoped that their children would all go into the business, though was not keen on the fact that there were a number of girls among his grand-children. Girls, he felt, were meant to be wives and mothers, and needn't be involved in business deals. His own sisters, both unmarried, he kept beside him as members of the board: he needed their votes in case his sons disagreed with his own ideas. This way, he still felt himself involved in the daily running. His sisters, he knew, were only interested in the money they gained each month from the dairy.

George came to, as his brother came into his office.

'You wanted to see me?'

'Wanted to run something past you. I'm desperately trying to think of some way to rid ourselves of the two yes-women on the Board. I wondered if you have any ideas? I don't think we're ever going to make progress until they're off.'

'You may be right, but I doubt Father would ever agree to them leaving.'

'Could we halve their votes? So they only make one vote between them?'

'Nice idea, but I doubt it. No, I fear we're saddled with them till they finally hang up their clogs. Father will always want them there so he can win whatever he wants to.' Henry was adamant and George had to agree with him.

'You're right, I suppose. Okay. The next deal I want to do . . . I was hoping to buy a couple of farms off two old men who want to retire. Mind you, I doubt the old man will allow that.'

'Can we afford them?'

'Oh, yes. I've actually spoken to them both. They seem quite happy with my offer. Though that won't be worth anything if he won't agree.'

'Put it to the Board. You never know your luck.'

They talked about the rest of the company. Henry was in charge of the bottling plant and was concerned about some of the workers.

'I'm afraid they're starting to get restless. Wanting more money. Any chance of giving them a raise?'

'It'll start a fashion. No, they'll have to wait till the year end. Heavens. We could all do with more money, couldn't we? How's young James getting on down there?'

'He's doing OK. I have him working alongside some of the old-timers. He quite likes it really. I'll move him on to join Philip in a couple of months.'

'Good. Looks as if Father will get his wishes to have the entire family in the business. Not so sure about my girls, mind you. Thank heavens we persuaded him to drop his plans to have one large house with all of us living together under the same roof. Can you just imagine it?'

'Hell on earth. You'd drive me mad if we lived even closer than we do.'

'On that note, let us get to work.'

Henry rose and left the room. He wondered exactly what his brother did all day, but as the company kept running along smoothly, he never asked. Since their father had more or less retired, George had taken over the reins, and it seemed the natural choice. Eldest brother and all that. The trouble with having such a large family was that everyone wanted their fingers in the pot. They'd all had to learn to accept one boss and live with that. His own two sons were entering the business and learning from the bottom up. George had two daughters, still in education. One of them, Georgia, was at university, learning something to do with arty stuff. He wasn't entirely certain what, but a degree was a degree in whatever subject. He wasn't sure where she would eventually fit into the dairy — or if she even wanted to. George's younger daughter, Maria, was studying for A-levels. He assumed she would go to university too, but nothing had been said about her future. He'd been disappointed when his own sons had turned down the chance of university, wanting to work in their grandfather's firm. He couldn't blame them, after listening to his father's diatribe about learning from the *university of life*. But they were both there and entering the long learning curve that seemed to be expected of them. Philip was working in the laboratory, where he was working on the various tests they needed to do on the milk; and James, his youngest, was working on the bottling plant's production line.

'How's it going, James?' he asked on his way through.

'Fine. I'm getting the hang of it now. Nothing too difficult. It's a matter of getting the rhythm going in time to the machine. Drive me bonkers to be doing this for much longer, mind you. Isn't there something else I can do?'

'I'll think about it. Carry on.' Henry smiled to himself as he walked away. Typical of these youngsters. Learn one thing and move on. Well, he needed to be there for a while longer. Maybe a spell out on the rounds would be good for him. They were a man down, after all. Yes, he would suggest that should be his next move. James was eighteen, after all; quite old enough to go out delivering milk. He was a fairly competent driver, having passed his driving test almost as soon as he was old enough. Henry would suggest it to George, to solve their immediate problems.

2

Georgia, named for her father, was having a wonderful time at university. Supposedly studying modern art, she and Giles, another student, had decided to spend a day at one of the galleries in London. Neither of them treated the day out very seriously; after a quick rush round the gallery, they were now sitting drinking large cups of frothy coffee in one of the many nearby coffee bars.

'Trouble with modern art — it's just too modern,' said Giles, rather pretentiously.

'Oh yes, indeed. I know exactly what you mean.' They both burst out laughing.

'I do like you, Georgia. I mean, really like you.'

'Oh Giles, I like you too. Really like you,' she said with a laugh.

'Jolly good. I mean . . . Would you . . . shall we go out together? You know, as a couple?'

'I thought we were. Can't see anyone else around, can you?'

'Excellent.' He reached over the table and took her hand. He lifted it to kiss and she blushed. 'I'll kiss you properly later.'

'I shall look forward to it. You've got a coffee moustache. You'd have to wipe it off first.'

'Have I? Does it suit me?'

'Don't ever grow a moustache. I'd hate you to look like my father. He has quite a bushy one and I don't like it at all.'

He wiped away the coffee and promised never to grow a moustache. 'So, when do I get to meet your parents?'

'My parents? Wow. I don't think that's a good idea at all.'

'Why ever not?'

'My mother is a . . . well, she's a total snob. My father is obsessed with milk.

No, I don't think it's a good idea. Sorry and all that.'

'You can meet my mother. She's reasonably friendly. In fact, I'd like you to meet her. I think you two have a lot in common.'

'Really? I'd like that. What's she like?'

'Wait and see. What shall we do now? It's actually beginning to rain out there.'

'Let's go to the cinema. There's a James Dean showing. I adore him.'

'What else is on?'

'*Blackboard Jungle*. It's supposed to be good. Maybe a bit worthy. I like the idea of *Rebel Without a Cause*.'

'Okay. We'll go and see that. Only one slight problem — I haven't brought enough money with me to treat you.'

'Don't be silly, I'll pay for us both. One good thing about having a father obsessed with milk, he does give me plenty of cash.'

'I don't like to think of you paying.'

'Don't be so old-fashioned. I really don't mind. It's only money. Daddy will give me some more if I ask him.'

'I can't imagine how that feels. My mother is never flush at all. She barely scrapes by, actually.'

'How awful for you. Even during the war I never remember feeling hungry. I think Daddy used to bring stuff home from the dairy to supplement the rations. Mind you, I was only small when it was all over. I remember learning about everything being fine after the *duration*. I always wondered what the 'duration' was. Some large man hovering over us, or something.'

'I remember everyone talking about it too. Well, we are both twenty, I suppose. We must have similar memories. Mind you, my father was killed, and everything changed after that. Mother had to go out and work, and give up on her painting for a while.'

'I didn't realise she painted. What sort of stuff does she paint?'

'Portraits mainly, when she can get a commission. She's pretty good. Hence my studying art; I grew up with a pencil in my hands. Anyway, are we going to see this film or not?'

They rose together and went off to find the cinema.

Sitting close to Georgia, Giles reached over and took her hand. She nestled against him, rather enjoying their vicarious pleasure of cinema during the afternoon.

'James Dean is so darned sexy,' Georgia sighed, after the film had finished.

'Doesn't do it for me,' laughed Giles.

'I'm glad about that. I need something to eat now. Come on, there's a place just along here. And don't worry, I'm buying.' He followed her, feeling somewhat uncomfortable. Maybe going out with her was not an option. He existed only on his grant and it only covered the basics.

'Look Georgia, I'm sorry, but this isn't going to work. I can't keep up with you. You have a really well-off family, and there's just me and my mother. I can't afford to eat out and go the cinema whenever the mood takes me. Don't argue with me. I know you have lots of money and I don't. I can't sponge off you. It goes against my nature.'

'Giles, please don't think like that. It's so silly. We enjoy each other's company, and I want us to stay friends and possibly something more. Just stop worrying about me paying. It's my father paying anyway. Can't you think of it like that?'

He sighed. He really liked this crazy girl and wanted to get to know her better. Could he swallow his pride and accept her terms?

'Maybe just this once. But it can't happen every time we want to spend time together. I'll have to get a job.'

'And then you'll never have enough time to spend with me. Come on. Let's go and eat, and no more arguments.' She swept along to the nearest cafe and ordered large portions of eggs and chips.

'I love eating here. It's so basic and my father would have a duck fit if he saw me eating like this. Good, isn't it?'

'Oh yes, indeed. You're completely mad you know.'

'Yes, I know. And you are completely

gorgeous. I really don't care if you're rich or poor. You are exactly right for me. You obviously had a good education, you speak nicely and are gorgeous-looking.'

'After all that, what can I say? How do I compare with Mr James Dean?'

'Oh, you beat him hollow. He isn't real, anyway; of course I know that. He's a big image that is created to fill the screen. You are real, and I like what I see. So, come on, if you've finished, let's go. I ought to think about going home pretty soon. It's getting pretty late. My parents will wonder what's happened to me.'

'I'll see you to your train. Tomorrow, we have to be in early. Come on.' He grabbed her hand and they went to the station. He kissed her goodbye and, glowing with pleasure, she went home. Life was going to be good, she decided.

'Hallo dear,' said her mother as she arrived home. 'You're late. Wherever have you been?'

'Oh, some of the college crowd were

eating out, so I went along with them. Sorry.'

'You might have let me know. I've kept some dinner for you. Your father was not pleased.'

'Sorry, I didn't think. I'll apologise to Daddy when I see him. Is Maria in her room?'

'She's doing her homework. At least I know where she is these days. It's a pity you can't live in at your college in London. At least I'd know when to cook or not.'

'I'll go and see Maria. *She'll* be pleased to see me, at least.'

'Don't be silly, dear. It's just rather inconvenient to prepare food that will be wasted. I do have other things to do with my life, you know.'

'Yes, Mother, I've said I'm sorry. Now, can I go and see my sister?'

'Oh, go on. But in future, let me know if you require a meal or not.'

As she ran upstairs, she heard her mother saying, '*Really*.' She knew she was in the wrong, but somehow she couldn't care less. She tapped on her sister's door and went into the room.

'Oh, hi there,' said Maria. 'Where were you this evening?'

'In Town, of course. I've got a new boyfriend. He's one of my group at Uni. Gorgeous to look at and very nice by nature. Don't tell Mother, though. She'll want to meet him and undoubtedly she'll consider him quite unsuitable. How was supper?'

'The usual sort of drag. Father complained pretty well all the time. You being missing didn't exactly help.'

'No wonder Mummy was so cross with me. We had double egg and chips in a sort of transport caff.'

'No wonder you thought Mummy would disapprove. Is that the best you could do?'

'I adore egg and chips. I can't imagine her ever cooking anything like that, can you?'

'No. We had some sort of casserole. I think it was chicken, but who knows? Probably beef.'

'She made it sound as if she'd made something specially for me. '*I have more to do in life than cook food that will be wasted*.'' Her impersonation of their mother was extremely accurate and both of them roared with laughter.

'I'd better get on. Must finish my essay before tomorrow.'

'Get on with it, child. I shall go and dream about Giles.'

'All right for some. Night, sister mine.'

'Night. May see you tomorrow. May not of course. Sweet dreams.'

Georgia went to her own room and flopped onto the bed. She closed her eyes and fell asleep within seconds. She awoke at some point and decided to crawl into her bed, fully-clothed.

The next morning, her mother came into her room to wake her, and she pulled the covers up round her neck so she wouldn't see.

'Come on, get up. You said you had an early start.'

'Okay. I'll get up.'

'Come on then, I want to see you.'

'I'll get up after you leave me. Go on. I promise I'll be up.'

'That is no way to speak to me. Really, I don't know where your manners have gone since you were at that dratted college of yours.'

'I'm growing up, Mother. Just growing up.'

'Well, let's hope you grow into some decent manners. Breakfast in five minutes.' She swept out of the room and Georgia sighed. Her mother was really quite impossible. She wondered about Giles' mother. She sounded quite fun. Maybe she would go and meet her soon. Make a change from her own parents at least. She rose and cast her dirty clothes down on the floor. A very quick splash under the shower and she dressed. She decided to wear one of her better dresses and hang several scarves round her neck. Her parents would certainly object but she felt it went with her new lifestyle.

'What on earth are you wearing? Take

those ridiculous scarves off right away. You look positively bohemian.' Her mother was furious.

'I don't see why. I'm over twenty years old. Nearly twenty-one, in fact. Much too ancient to be told what to do. I'm thinking of looking for somewhere to stay in London. Will you help me, Daddy? Paying for it, I mean.'

'Nonsense. You've got a season ticket I bought for you. Why on earth do you want the expense of living there? No chance, I'm afraid. Time you started to realise money doesn't grow on trees.'

'Comes out of milk bottles, doesn't it?' she said cheekily.

'It may do, but no way am I going to pay for a flat or anything for you to live in. I'd better be off. We've got no end of problems at the dairy. Some of the staff are threatening strike action; I need to sort them out first thing. Won't be in for lunch, dear.'

'That's nothing new. I can't remember the last time I did lunch for you.' Nicola sniffed as she spoke.

'I, at least, tell you these things. Unlike some members of this family.'

'I've already said how sorry I am. Please can we let the subject drop now?' Georgia was sick of it. 'Did you get your essay finished, Maria?'

'Just about. I was going to copy it out again, but they'll have to put up with it as it is. They should be able to read it, so why worry?'

'Not the right attitude, my girl,' said George as he was leaving. 'Make sure it is legible before you hand it in. I want at least one of my daughters to enter a sensible course at university. This art nonsense is going nowhere. I'll be glad when you've finished the course and I can have you at the dairy where I can keep my eye on you.'

'As if . . . ' Georgia told him. 'I shall go off and live in a garret with a man of my choice. I shall paint exotic pictures all day and make love all night.'

'Where on earth do you get these ideas?' her mother retorted. 'I've never heard anything like it. Now, eat up your breakfast and get yourself ready for university. And Maria, get yourself off to school.' The two girls pulled faces at their mother behind her back and giggled. 'Now what's amusing you?' she snapped.

'I'm going now,' Georgia said. 'I won't be in for dinner.'

'Where are you going?'

'There an exhibition I want to see. I'll grab something en route. Bye now.'

'That girl,' her mother grumbled.

'She's finding her feet. Don't obsess about it. And don't worry. She'll find someone and get married before you know it. And I'll be away at Uni too, so you can have the entire house to yourself.'

'But surely you'll go to London University.'

'Not if I have the choice. Another year and I finish my A-levels. Then it's off to the bright lights of Leeds or Manchester — or even Oxford or Cambridge, if I'm good enough.'

'Now you are being ridiculous.'

'Bye, Mummy. See you tonight.'

Nicola slumped down at the table again. She had a whole day ahead of her with no-one to talk to. Well, apart from Mrs Henders, and she was hardly a font of good conversation. She sighed, wondering what she might do with herself. Thank goodness for her radio. She could listen to *Woman's Hour*, and then there was usually a good play in the afternoon. Perhaps she might turn out her wardrobe. There were lots of things she'd never wear again.

She went upstairs and into Georgia's room, saw the clothes lying in a heap on the floor, and cursed her daughter yet again. She had a good mind to leave them where they were; but then Mrs Henders wouldn't be able to clean. With a sigh, she picked them up and hung them in her wardrobe. The dirty things she dropped into the laundry basket for Mrs Henders to put into the machine later. She hated her life at the moment. She really wished for something like the dairy to occupy her thoughts. She went downstairs and dialled one of her sisters-in-law. A good moan to one of them was exactly what she needed.

★ ★ ★

George walked through the bottling plant and wondered how any of them could stand the racket. It was all moving smoothly and the machines were passing the bottles along in lines, just as they should. He watched as they were first blown through with steam to sterilise them and then tipped over to dry. By the time they had travelled in their own lines along to the milk supply, they had cooled down, and were turned again to await the milk to be poured into them. Once filled, another short journey to the capping process. Each bottle was raised to the machine; then, with a brief blast, the caps were fitted. After this, they passed a little further to where a couple of men stood putting them into crates. It was a simple process and all seemed to be working perfectly.

George nodded to the workers as he passed them. He spoke to James to ask how things were going.

'Okay. I'm looking forward to my next move,' he shouted, to make himself heard above the racket.

'I'll speak to your father later.'

'Great.' They nodded at each other and George walked on out of the plant to the relative peace of the laboratories. Here he met up with Henry's eldest, Philip.

'What are you working on?' he asked the young man.

'Morning, sir. I'm looking at the TB tests we carry out. We're wondering if we should make some changes.'

'Excellent. Carry on the good work.'

He went on to his office. It seemed all was well as far as he could see. He glanced through the rest of his mail and handed it to his secretary to do the letters. She would doubtless make her usual good job of them and return the letters for him to sign later.

George leaned back in his chair and

contemplated his next move. He started making notes on how to remove his father from the board — and got nowhere. As if on cue, his father came into the office.

Geoffrey was a grand old man of — though he denied this, of course — eighty-one. He was tall, had a thick crop of grey hair, and looked almost majestic standing at the door of the office.

'Morning, my boy,' he said in a commanding tone.

'Oh, Father. Good morning. Come and sit down.' His father stood a moment longer, as if deciding where to sit; sighed, and sat in the chair opposite the desk.

'Not used to sitting this side of the desk yet. I suppose it will come eventually. How are things going?'

'All on target. As usual of course.'

'Sales up?'

'About the same as usual. The shops are doing quite well. We're thinking of expanding the one here, if we can decide on how to make the space. It's one of the first self-service shops in the area.'

'I trust it will be on the agenda for the Board meeting next week?'

'I don't think there's much discussion needed, actually. Henry and I have already talked it over, and more or less decided on how it can be done.'

'Oh, no. Not good enough. We need to discuss it *thoroughly*. Your Aunts may have their thoughts on how it may be expanded; you need to listen to their ideas, you know. They have many things to contribute.'

'And many spokes to put into the wheels,' he muttered.

'What did you say?'

'Nothing. Just thinking aloud.'

'Well, make sure it goes onto the agenda. When can we expect to receive it? The agenda, I mean.'

'Towards the end of the week, I should think.'

'Good. Make sure it's with us by Friday at the latest. Now, how is young Philip doing?'

'I think he's found his niche. He's still in the labs at the moment. Seems to be working quite well, in fact. I called in on him today.'

'Good. And the other one?'

'James? He's still in the bottling plant. He's ready to move on.'

'Don't hurry him through the processes. He needs to spend time in each department and get a thorough grounding in every process.'

'Yes, Father. I remember it well.'

'Yes, so you should. I need you to be able to take over, whenever necessary, anywhere in the dairy.'

'You need me? I thought you'd retired.'

'Hmm. Yes, well, I suppose I have. But it's good to know you're able to do as I said.'

They talked for a while and at last Geoffrey decided to leave.

'I'll walk you out, shall I?'

'No, it's fine. I shall look at the various plants on my way. Make sure everything is up to scratch. I'll probably come over to you for Sunday lunch.'

'Very well, Father. We'll see you on Sunday.' He felt somewhat resigned to his father's visits to his home. He must remember to tell Nicola.

'Make sure everyone's present. Long time since I saw your eldest.'

'I can't guarantee she'll be there. She's a bit of a wild card these days.'

'I've made my point. I want to see her on Sunday. Make sure she's there.' He walked out of George's office and slammed the door.

George sighed. Would the old man ever hand over control completely? Somehow, he doubted it.

3

Georgia had enjoyed her morning at University. One of the more interesting lecturers had just finished his talk on modern artists and their environment. She spoke to Giles after the lecture.

'I wish I'd taken more notice of the exhibition yesterday. He made some interesting points, didn't he?'

'We could always go again. See it with a different perspective. I'd never thought about some of the things he mentioned.'

'Watch it. You'll be a fan before you know it. I can see you actually liking some of the stuff we saw yesterday. But you're right, of course. We can go and look for traces of their background in the paintings. Some of them are easier than others. You know, what we really need is to actually go to Paris, and look at some of their art.'

'Oh, yes; and how do I afford that little outing? And, no thanks. You won't be paying for me to go with you.'

'Oh, well. Nice idea. I somehow doubt my dear father would pay for me to go anyway. Maybe we could go in the Vac. We could get jobs and spend the whole summer there.'

'My mother has asked if you'd like to come to our place on Sunday. Will you come?'

'Oh, I don't know. But thank her from me.' She thought about it for a while. 'Yes, I think I will. Be something to look forward to. Tell me your address. I'll see if I can borrow Mummy's car and then I can drive there: the roads are never too bad on a Sunday.'

'We have a flat in Highgate. Well, it was all our house once when my father was alive. Mum sold it off in stages, and we just have the ground floor left. It is very nice, actually. I think you'll like it.'

'I shall look forward to it. Now, are we going back to the gallery? I feel I can look at some of the paintings with a little more insight.'

He smiled and took her hand. 'Come on, then. Let's walk there. It's a nice morning.'

Giles asked her about the dairy as they walked. She told him of her grandfather's dream to give employment to the whole family.

'Two of my cousins work there already. Neither of them went to university, but just straight there. I think he was disappointed that my father had two daughters. He isn't sure women can do anything but secretarial work, so I may be off the hook. Though doubtless he expects me to be married and have hordes of babies. Be a *proper woman*, of course.' She said this as a passable imitation of her grandfather, though Giles wouldn't have recognised it.

'You sound rather bitter about him.'

'No, not really. He's always been quite a sweetie to me, but thinks my going to Uni was a waste of time as I'm only a girl. He thinks I'll just get married, and then the expense of my education will be wasted.'

'But you don't think like that, I take it?'

'Course not. No education is a waste of time. I may not do anything with it, but I'm having a ball. Don't tell him that, though.'

'Not very likely I'll ever meet him.'

'I'll give it some thought. Golly, how much further is it?'

They continued to walk, chatting easily. Once they arrived at the gallery, they went inside with a new attitude to the paintings. It was a useful exercise, and both of them felt good by the time they had finished.

'I'm going to buy you a coffee today,' Giles told her. 'Come on. Our favourite coffee bar is along here.' She didn't argue, and they sat close together until the frustrated waitress came over and told them they must re-order or leave. Apologetically, they rose; and, still holding on to each other, left and walked slowly back towards the station.

'Oh, heavens. I told my mother I'd be out for dinner this evening.'

'I'm afraid I'm expected back at home.'

'No worries. I'll grab a sandwich at the station.'

'If you're sure. I'd better go now or I'll be very late.' He leaned over and kissed her. She felt the world rock slightly and then came to.

'Wow,' she managed to utter. 'That was quite something.'

'I agree. I shall look forward to lots more of those. See you tomorrow. I'll tell Mum you're coming on Sunday; she'll be delighted.'

Georgia floated home, realising she had quite forgotten about getting anything to eat. When she arrived, the family were sitting at the table.

'Oh, Georgia. I wasn't expecting you. I haven't cooked for you.'

'No, I know I said I'd be out. The plans didn't work out. I'll make a sandwich. Don't worry about it.'

'But you can't exist on a sandwich. It

isn't good for you.'

'Just eat your own meal, Mummy. I'll be fine.' She went into the kitchen and decided on toasted cheese. She sat there to eat it, and when her mother came in, she had almost finished.

'Oh. You've finished the cheese.'

'Sorry. Is that a problem?'

'I suppose not. Your father can always bring some more back tomorrow.'

'It's very convenient having a dairy, isn't it?'

'I'm not sure what you mean.'

'Run out of anything from their shop and Daddy can bring more home. I wonder how poor people manage to keep supplies going.'

Her mother glared at her. 'Your grandfather is coming to lunch on Sunday. He particularly asked that you be there.'

'I'm sorry, but I'm going out for lunch.'

'On Sunday?' she said in shocked tones. 'But you can't. I'm sorry, but you are always here on Sundays. Your grandfather has especially . . . '

'I know, especially asked for me to be here. Well, I'm sorry, but it's been arranged for ages. I'm going to a friend's house. Some work we need to do together. I'll see Grandfather another time.'

'He won't be pleased. Not at all. I don't suppose your father will be either.'

Her father came into the kitchen. 'Are we having dessert or not?' he demanded.

'Sorry. I was telling Georgia she's expected here on Sunday when your father comes for lunch. She says she's arranged to go out.'

'Well, she can just un-arrange it. She is required to be here. Now, dessert?'

'He can't do this to me,' she exploded when he had left the room. 'I'm going out anyway. I shall be twenty-one in a few weeks. Then I'll show him independence.'

'You still need his support for university, don't forget. You'd have to leave if he doesn't pay your expenses. I'd better take dessert in. Do you want some?'

'Not really. I'm going up to my room

now. I've got some work to finish.'

'Georgia, please don't upset your father so much. It won't do you any good in the long run.'

'I'm sorry, but I must go out on Sunday. I told him I would, and he was so pleased.'

'He? Who is this?'

'Nobody you know. I'll see you tomorrow.' She ran upstairs to her room and shut the door. Suddenly, Sunday had become terribly important to her.

She lay on her bed and listened to the family noises below. She heard her mother (she assumed it was her mother) washing up, and her father put on the television. She heard her sister come upstairs to her room and switch her radio on. Radio Luxembourg, she assumed from the music that came through. She got up and sat at her desk, taking some papers out and trying to look at her notes. The trouble was, she kept on thinking about Giles' kiss.

She smiled and wrapped her arms round herself. Her first real kiss. Of course, she'd been kissed before, but never like that. Usually, it was inexperienced fumblings after dances. Worthy suitors introduced by her parents. Boys her father approved of: boys she could never like very much.

Giles was everything she could want. He might not have any money to spare, but he was gorgeous. Good-looking and funny, and he obviously cared for her. She had high hopes of her relationship with this one, and if her parents didn't approve, then so be it. It was her life, not theirs. She really didn't care about having money. She'd live in the proverbial garret with Giles . . . Heavens, she was now getting rather carried away!

Her mother knocked on her door.

'I need to speak to you, dear,' she said on entering. 'Who is this person you're going to see on Sunday?'

'Just someone from college,' she replied, thinking how much more he was.

'Name?'

'Giles. He's just another student in my year group.'

'And where does this Giles live?'

'Highgate.'

'Does he live on his own or with others?'

'With others,' she lied. Her mother would never understand if she told her that he lived with his mother. 'It's a flat they have. I'm going, Mummy. Whatever you say. I was going to ask if I could borrow your car, but I suppose that's out of the question.'

'Oh no, certainly not. You can't borrow my car.'

'Okay, I'll go by train. No problem. I'll have to leave quite early to get there in time, but no worries. Now, if you'll excuse me, I have an essay to finish.' Her mother left with a deep sigh. She grinned to herself after she'd left. It did feel rather wicked lying like that; but if it meant she could spend a whole day with Giles, why should she worry? She tried to settle down to some work.

Downstairs, her mother spoke to her father.

'I can't persuade Georgia to stay at

home on Sunday, I'm afraid.'

'You're too soft with her. I'll tell her she'll be there. When my father makes his demands, he expects them to be carried out. Don't I know it. Do you know, we have all agreed on expanding the shop — worked out how to do it and exactly where to put it — and now he wants that on the agenda for the board meeting. Wants to discuss it all and give his approval or not.'

'Oh dear. That will be difficult.'

'He'll bring in his wretched sisters who will agree with him, and I doubt very much we shall be altering anything. I really feel very angry about it.'

'I'm so sorry, dear. Perhaps he'll surprise you and agree to it.'

'Oh, I doubt that. He'll want a vote on it; and then, when the votes are equal, he'll take on the role of Chairman of the Board and have the casting vote. He's done it so many times before, I don't see this being any different. He objects to us making any decisions without his blessing.'

'I suppose it gives him something to think about. He may have retired from the running of the place but he still wants to be involved.'

'He's got a lot worse since Mother died. I suppose he must be missing her. She was always the voice of reason.'

'Must be nearly a year since she passed on.'

'Died. Say died. I hate the term *passed on*. She is dead: that's it, and all about it.'

Nicola said nothing more. She settled down to watch television. George was asleep in the next few minutes so she felt she could actually relax and enjoy the programme.

She thought about her life. She had everything she could want except good company. The girls were both almost grown up, though really she doubted that about her elder daughter. She had all the help she could possibly want in keeping the house clean and tidy. All she had to do all day was plan and cook the evening meal. She didn't even really have to go shopping for it, as the butcher delivered and there were vegetables in the garden, brought in by the gardener.

She had worked a little during the war. She had fond memories of driving a large van around, delivering waste to a farm for the pigs. She'd blessed her own father for teaching her to drive at a young age: at least it gave her something to do each day. Her husband and one of his brothers were in a reserved occupation, running the dairy. His youngest brother Michael had gone away to war towards the end, but had returned unharmed, much to all their reliefs. Now, she was left with little to do and too much time to do it in. Apart from her radio, her days seemed empty. Her life felt empty. She needed to do something.

George awoke.

'Think I'm going to turn in now. Are we having a drink?'

'What do you want?'

'Cocoa, I think.'

'Very well. I'll go and make it.'
Typical George. Demand something
and she leapt up to get it. She made
two cups and took them into the
lounge. 'Here you are.'

'Girls not having any?'

'I doubt it. I think they've both gone
to bed. Oh, we need more cheese
tomorrow. Can you bring it?'

'I suppose so. Remind me again
tomorrow.' They drank their cocoa and
went up to bed. 'Don't forget to tell
Georgia she will be here on Sunday,' he
said as he lay down.

'I'll try. Don't hold out much hope,
though . . . ' But he'd fallen asleep
instantly. Lucky him, Nicola thought.

By Friday, the agenda was com-
pleted. George had included the plans
for the extension to the shop plus the
rest of the details to be discussed. He'd
asked Michael to deliver it to his father
and Aunts; he couldn't face seeing
them at the moment. Whyever had his
father retired and handed over to him
as the Managing Director, and yet

wanted to keep such a tight rein on everything they did? The day drifted by and soon it was time to go home. His secretary came in to say his wife had telephoned and asked her to remind him about cheese.

'Oh lord. Yes, I'd forgotten about that. Thank you. Have a nice weekend.'

'Thank you, sir. I'm not doing anything special but it will be nice to have a break.'

He paused, wondering what on earth his secretary did with herself.

'Thank you,' he repeated. She left the room, and he collected things together and went into the shop. He picked up a piece of cheese and put it into his briefcase; he never thought of paying for it. He picked up some eggs at the same time and carried them out to his car, looking forward to a day in the garden tomorrow. He might offer to take his wife out for supper as well. It would be a good weekend, he felt sure.

Georgia was taking down instructions

to find Giles' home. She would have to go by train as her mother was certainly not receptive to lending her the car. Pity, but she felt sure she would manage it.

'What time will you be here?' Giles asked her.

'When do you want me?'

'Seven o'clock would be lovely.'

'Seven? I thought you'd asked me for lunch?'

'In the morning. Then you can have breakfast too.' They both laughed. 'Come when you like. Any time after eleven.'

'Okay. Look out for me around eleven, I'm sure I can make it by then. I said Mummy doesn't want to lend me her car. There's some family thing going on and she wants me to be there, but I've said no. Your invitation came first.'

'Mum would be very disappointed not to meet you. She's looking forward to it. I've told her all about you.'

'Not all, I hope.'

'I told her what a magic kisser you

are, and how you wrinkle your nose when you're concentrating.'

'Oh Giles, I don't, do I? Anyway, I don't believe you.'

'Mum is quite bohemian. I told you she paints. She may be doing so on Sunday, and will probably be covered in paint and won't have anything ready for you.'

'Interesting. I shall look forward to seeing her work. I suppose I should go home now.'

'I suppose I should too. It means leaving you, though. You don't know how hard that is.'

'Oh Giles.' She reached over to him and kissed him. 'It's hard for me too. You're my first real boyfriend.'

'And you're my first real girlfriend.' They both laughed. 'I'll walk you to the station.' He put his arm round her and they walked along slowly, stopping every now and then for another kiss. 'You're quite addictive, you know.'

'My father would have a duck fit if he saw us kissing like this. Something one keeps for the privacy of one's room, don't you know.' He laughed at her impersonation again.

'I look forward to meeting him one day. He sounds extremely pompous.'

'Oh, he is. But with Grandfather around all the time, it's hardly surprising. He retired a few years ago, but Daddy seems frightened of him still — he's MD of the company, but he still has to kowtow to him. Pardon the pun! *Cow* . . . oh, well. There's a board meeting next week so he's already going downhill fast.'

'I don't know anything about companies and boards. I think my father was a teacher. I didn't really know him. He was killed in the war, must be at least twelve years ago now.'

'I'm sorry.'

'Oh, don't be. Mum and I get along pretty well. No real demands on each other. We're more like friends than a parent and son.'

'How amazing. My parents both expect me to be a dutiful daughter, respectful at all times. They're not so bad really. I just wish Mummy would relax a bit. I really don't know what she does with herself all day. I know she likes *Woman's Hour* and radio plays, but Mrs Henders comes in every day to clean. I suppose she has the evening meal to do, and lunches when we're all at home.'

'I can't imagine what it's like to have regular meals. I mean, meals at particular times. It's all pretty erratic at our place. But don't worry, Sunday lunch will be served at *some* point. May not be till two o'clock, but it will be there. And probably something good. When she tries, she's a pretty good cook. Well, here we are.'

'I'll see you on Sunday then.' She kissed him and left him standing on the platform as she ran along to catch her train. She turned to wave but he had left. She sat down and reflected on the week. It had been quite a time. She felt happier than she had for ages. She now had a boyfriend and was like most other girls of her age. She couldn't help grinning to herself as she sat there. She saw a woman opposite staring at her and smiled once more. Couldn't the woman see how good life was?

4

Saturday seemed endless and rather boring. It was a sunny day and Georgia's father had come home early from his stint at the dairy. He went straight outside, and spent much of the day in the garden. Nicola listlessly prepared something for them to eat at lunchtime, and then again for dinner in the evening. The rest of the day, she wandered in and out and picked some flowers. She watched her husband as he worked in the greenhouse.

'Couldn't Bill do that for you?' she asked.

'Well, perhaps he could. But I quite enjoy pottering around. Nothing too strenuous, of course. I'll leave him a list of what I want him to do later this week.'

She wandered back into the house and sighed. She didn't even get her husband's company at the weekends.

The girls were equally missing from her circuit. She went upstairs to see what they were doing.

'Oh, there you are,' she said. 'I wondered what you were doing.'

'Just chatting. Do you want something?' replied Georgia, who was busily planning her outfit for the next day.

'I'd quite like a chat myself.' She sounded rather wistful and Maria felt slightly guilty.

'Come and sit by me. I'm sure you can add your advice.' Georgia looked at her sister as if looks could kill. 'What? What have I said?'

'Nothing. It's okay.'

Nicola sat down beside her daughters, and there was a silence. Nobody could think of anything to say.

'Advice about what?' she asked after a minute or two.

'Clothes, of course. She doesn't know what to wear tomorrow.'

'I didn't realise it was so important, dear. Aren't you going to some student digs to work?'

Maria laughed. 'Is that what she said?'

Nicola looked puzzled. 'Well, where are you going?'

'To see her boyfriend.'

'Oh, I see. I didn't know she even *had* a boyfriend. Your grandfather is expecting you to be here, and your father has asked me to make sure you are.'

'I won't be, I'm afraid. Tell him I'm sorry.'

'So where are you going?'

'I told you. Highgate.'

'I suppose that's reasonably respectable, if it's the right area. So who lives in this student flat?'

'She's going to meet his mother. He lives with his mother. His father died during the war.' Maria was proving a vast source of information.

'I see,' replied their mother, who was by now feeling somewhat frustrated by all this news. 'So why haven't you invited him to visit us here?'

Georgia looked at her as if that was enough to explain. There was a silence.

'And have Daddy ranting on about

60

his precious dairy, and you sitting making small talk? No thanks.'

'Don't forget, that same *precious dairy* is the means by which you two have had a decent education and we live in a very nice house.'

'Shame about the relationship then, isn't it?'

'I'm not listening to any more of this.' She got up and left the two girls. Really, the ingratitude of her daughters never ceased to amaze her.

'Thanks a bunch, sister dear. You completely blew my cover story. Now she's gone away feeling all hurt and misunderstood. You can surely see why I didn't want to invite Giles here.'

'I don't really. They'd make him very welcome, I'm sure. Maybe it's too early in the relationship to bring him home. Oh, no — you're going to *his* home, aren't you?'

Georgia glared at her sister and continued to take more clothes out of her extensive wardrobe. Maria was soon bored, and got up and left her sister to it. Whatever she said would be wrong, so best to let Georgia make her own decisions. She went downstairs to find her mother. At least she would stay on good terms with her parents.

Georgia finally decided on a collection of clothes. Wanting to look particularly bohemian herself, she chose bright colours and put them together in various ways so the colours clashed. She liked the effect, and hope Giles' mother would too. She draped a couple of scarves round her neck, and looked quite striking — or so she thought. She would wear her newest long boots, though they weren't terribly comfortable. Still, what did that matter? They looked good. It was all about looking fashionable and stylish. Would Giles like the effect? Of course he would.

She laid her things out on a chair and sat down at her desk. Taking out her notes on the exhibition, she began her essay on *Modern Artists and Their Environment*. Was that the right title? She really couldn't remember.

The day dragged on. She went down for lunch and chatted to the family reasonably well. Her father said he was expecting she'd come to her senses and would obey his father's request. She made no reply to him.

'Well? Are you staying in as I've asked?'

'I'm sorry, Daddy; no. I made my arrangements before I knew about the imperial command.'

'So where are you going to exactly?'

She'd had enough. Maria had certainly let the cat out of the bag.

'I'm going for lunch at my boyfriend's house. With his mother. All right? His name is Giles and we've been seeing other at college since I started. Is that enough for you?' She got up and left the table, sobbing.

'Georgia. Come back here at once!' her father shouted after her retreating figure. They heard her run upstairs and her door slam. 'Really,' George said angrily. 'Daughters. Who'd have 'em?'

He left the table and went into his

study. He was furious to have lost the battle. And somehow he had to explain to his father why his daughter was missing tomorrow. He sat back in his chair and closed his eyes. He was only fifty-four and felt as if he had the cares of the world resting on his shoulders. The dairy certainly seemed to rest on him, and now he had a daughter who was proving the sort of responsibility he hadn't expected. He thought she would finish her degree, then come into the dairy for a year or two before marrying someone suitable. Someone local who would make a good match for her. Now she was going out with some boy from who knew where. Perhaps it was time to stand up to his father and tell him what he really thought of him. But then, he knew he'd never have the courage to do that.

After her stormy exit from the lunch table, Georgia lay on her bed. She felt a headache coming on and closed her eyes. It was the stress of living with her wretched family. It really was time she found somewhere to live on her own or with some people of her own age. But how could she afford that? She could always manage on her allowance, but the cost of renting somewhere in London would completely break the bank. She eventually fell into a doze, and dreamt of Giles asking her to marry him and her grandfather stopping the wedding at the last minute.

Maria helped her mother to clear up the lunch things. It had only been a cold meal with meat and salad.

'Wash or dry?' she asked.

'Really don't mind, dear. You go and get on with your work if you want to. I've got nothing else to do all afternoon. Except prepare dinner, of course, and maybe do something towards tomorrow. Actually, that's quite a lot. You wash, I'll dry.'

'What are we having?'

'Roast beef, of course. What else would I serve to your grandfather?'

'Of course. Why did I ask? And apple pie for pudding?'

'Of course. I must check with Daddy that he's got your grandfather's favourite wine too. In fact, we'd better make sure there are two bottles in case he's in that sort of mood.'

'Must be tough for Daddy. At the dairy, I mean. He's in charge but still has to do what his father tells him.'

'You've no idea. Of course, I only get his side of the story, but I do know that Geoffrey is a pretty strong character.'

'I suppose he must have been to do all he has. How old is he now?'

'Eighty-one. At least he was persuaded to move into a smaller house after your grandmother died; it stopped him trying to persuade all of us to move in with him. They did all live there once, of course; but when George and I married, we'd already decided to move out. We rented somewhere for a while before buying this place. Grandfather thought we were mad, but thank heavens we did.'

'I can't imagine us all living in that great barn of a place. He's much better off living round the corner, even if it is a bit close. There, I've finished. Do you want me to peel some potatoes for dinner?'

'I thought we'd have rice, actually. Goes well with chicken casserole, I always feel. I must put that together now or it won't be done. Will you call in on Georgia? See if she's okay after her blast at lunchtime.'

'Sure. I think it's quite a new thing — this 'her and Giles' thing. She's actually quite nervous about it all.'

'Thank you, darling. You're a real comfort to me.'

'I'm glad. I haven't got my own life yet. I'll probably turn into a monster too, in another three years.'

'I wouldn't say she's a monster exactly, just reaching a difficult age. I suppose I've been lucky to have you both at home for so long.'

'It's a lovely home to be in. I'll go and talk to Georgia now.'

Maria ran upstairs and knocked on her sister's door. 'It's only me, Georgia.'

She opened it as quietly as she could and saw her sister asleep. She closed the door again and went to her own room. It woke the sleeping girl and she sat up.

'Maria?' she called out. Her sister came back.

'Sorry. I didn't mean to wake you,' she said as she came into the room. 'How are you now? That was quite a show you put on.'

'I feel pretty drained, actually. I'm not really this confrontational. I was just sick of being questioned about my life. I'm thinking of moving out. I need some space, but then I can't afford a flat of my own. I'm stuck here.'

'You're not that far from the end of your course. What is it, two more months? Three?'

'I suppose so. Then I'll have to get a job of some sort. Perhaps then I'll be able to afford my own place. I'll look for a job miles away from here and the dairy and everything that goes with it.'

'Best of luck with it. What sort of thing will you look for?'

'I have no idea. None at all.'

'So you have about three months to consider.'

'Heavens, you're right. I suppose I'll be looking for something in an art gallery or a museum, perhaps. Oh, I don't know. Maybe I should stay at Uni for another year. I really don't know. Something to think seriously about.'

They chatted on for the rest of the afternoon, talking about this and that.

'Thanks for being my sister, Maria. You talk a lot of sense, and I suspect you are older than your years suggest. Where did you learn to be so wise?'

'Who can tell? It must come naturally to me. Either that or it's studying the Ancient Greek philosophers.'

'Don't tell me you actually understand all of that stuff?'

'I'm pretty good at conning people. And I am doing my A-levels in the Classics.'

'You really are much brighter than I am. I got enough to get to Uni, but only in bread-and-butter subjects.'

'It got you to where you wanted to be. You'll pass easily. Then, with a degree, doors open for you. It's your twenty-first next month. What do you want for that?'

'I don't know. Depends on the parents' mood, I suppose.'

'I think they're planning a big party. Inviting the cousins and several other eligible men.'

'Sounds awful. I wonder if they'd give me money instead? Then I could pay a deposit on a flat.'

'Doubt that. No fun in it for them. No, I think you'll have to put up with a family do. Plus . . . '

'I know, several suitable bachelors. God, they are so boring. Now, scoot. We have to get ready for dinner.'

Father seemed to have restored his equilibrium and seemed in quite a good mood. Nicola also seemed reasonably calm, so dinner passed without incident.

'It's your twenty-first next month, dear. Thought we'd talk about who you want to invite. We'll get caterers, of course. Don't want your mother having to do everything.' He smiled benignly at his wife.

'Oh, I don't know. I wondered if I might go out with the college crowd.'

'Of course you won't. We'll have all the family, naturally.' The two girls exchanged glances. 'Your cousins will all be there, and their parents. If there's anyone else you want to invite, give their names and addresses to your mother. She can then decide if they are suitable.'

'We should invite some of the people you met at the Hunt Ball last year. Very suitable young men, in my opinion.'

'Invite whoever you like,' Georgia said, suddenly wearied by the whole idea. 'If I can't spend it with people I like, it makes no difference to me.'

'Now then, Georgia. No need to be so ungrateful. We also thought of buying you a nice piece of jewellery. A necklace or something.'

'Doubt I'll ever have the occasion to wear it.'

'Oh, but I thought we'd talked about

getting her a . . . ' Her father stopped. 'No, of course not. Just an idea I'd had.' His wife looked at him, shaking her head. Georgia saw this exchange but decided to let it pass. The subject was dropped.

They watched television for the evening and then she went up to her room. She felt excited at the prospect of tomorrow, and lay awake for some time. She also felt slightly nervous. She was going to Giles' house and going to meet his mother. She wondered what she looked like, imagining a sort of female version of him. She hoped the clothes she had chosen would be suitable; and, well after midnight, got up and went to her wardrobe. She hauled out a couple more items and tried them on. They'd do at a pinch. Then she put on her collection of mixed colours and looked at herself in the mirror. She quite liked the effect, but then decided it was too much.

She slumped down on her bed. If she only knew what Giles' mother was really like. She'd know easily what to wear. Maybe she should play it safe ... She dumped her things on the floor, chose a simple dress that she knew her mother would approve of, and put a scarf or three with it. If Giles' mum turned out to be some sort of exotic bohemian, she would leave them on. If she was a bit more normal, she'd take them off. Having finally decided, she settled down and went off to sleep.

After her disturbed night, she didn't wake till almost nine o'clock. She leapt out of bed and rushed into the shower, cursing everyone madly. She washed her hair and came out looking for her hair dryer.

'Maria? Have you got my hair dryer?' she bellowed.

'In my room,' she called back.

'What's it doing there? You've no right to borrow my stuff without asking.' She ran along to her sister's room and grabbed the dryer. Her hair was long and straight and took a lot of drying. It was getting later and later. At last it was dry, and she dressed in her newer outfit, grabbed her bag and went downstairs.

'Good. Your breakfast's ready,' her mother told her.

'Haven't time. I'll miss my train.'

'Really, Georgia. You must eat. Come and sit down. And why are you wearing that odd assortment of scarves? Take them off. It quite spoils the look of that dress.'

'I really don't have time to eat. I'll eat some toast. I can eat that walking along to the station. There aren't all that many trains on a Sunday. If I miss this one, I shall be late arriving.'

'If I do lend you my car, will you eat some breakfast?'

'Oh Mummy, really? Yes, of course I'll eat my breakfast. It does look good.'

'Well, as long as you promise to look after it. No dumping it in a side street. If they don't have parking space, you must leave it in a car park near to where they live. Understand?'

'Yes, Mummy. Thank you so much.

Gosh, this is lovely,' she said, tucking into her bacon and eggs. Thank you. Is that coffee? I'd love some, please.'

'If this is what happens when I loan you my car, I should do it more often. Do you know the way to go?'

'Yes, of course. It won't take me too long to drive there. Giles gave me a map of his road. Oh lord, I haven't put it in my bag.' She leapt up from the table and ran upstairs to find it. 'Got it. Now, where's that coffee?'

Less than half an hour later, she was on the road. She really thought she knew exactly where to go, and drove very carefully to Highgate. She was quite near to his house, she thought. She stopped in the street, looking again at his drawing and the name of the street she was in.

'Don't panic,' she told herself. 'It can't be far away.' She rummaged in the glove box and found a rather elderly A to Z. The page she needed was torn in half. 'Damnation,' she breathed. Then she realised that Giles' directions led from the Underground station. She drove slowly round, looking for the sign. There it was, only she was going in the opposite direction. Then she realised she had driven right past his house. It was a much larger and grander house than she'd expected. Much bigger than their house in Barnet. There was a large drive in front and she drove in. It was now almost half-past eleven. She knocked at the door and waited.

5

A short, plumpish lady came to the door. She was wearing a black dress, long and somewhat stained with paint, and looked younger than what must have been her age. Late forties? Early fifties? She looked nothing at all like Giles, having dark hair and — well, being rather short.

'Hallo, dear. You must be Georgia.'

'Mrs Hoburn?'

'Come on in. I'm afraid Giles has gone to meet you. You must have missed him. He'll be at the station, no doubt. Come in and have some coffee.'

'Thank you. Should I go and look for him? I borrowed my mother's car and drove here. I didn't tell him, so . . . well, I suppose that's why he was expecting me by train.'

'Have some coffee, and if he isn't back then you can go and meet him.

You look very nice, dear. He has described you very well.'

'Thank you,' Georgia replied uncertainly. She felt uncomfortable talking to this stranger without Giles being there. 'He has told me lots about you too. You paint, don't you?'

'I dabble. Well, yes of course, I paint. In fact, I'm quite obsessive about painting. But I expect he's told you that too. I have actually put lunch together today. That's quite an effort for me.'

'Oh, well thank you.' She wondered what on earth the lady had *put together*. She poured a cup of the strongest coffee Georgia had ever tasted.

'Milk? Help yourself.' She did, liberally.

It turned out to be quite delicious so she commented about it.

'My own recipe. Freshly ground coffee with a touch of this and that.'

'It looks very strong but it isn't bitter at all. Lovely.'

There was a noise in the hall. Giles had returned.

'Oh, there you are. I was giving up on you.'

'Mummy lent me her car in the end. I'm sorry I didn't let you know.' He leaned over and kissed her. She blushed, aware of his mother standing nearby.

'You look nice,' he told her. 'Makes a change from the college outfits. I like it.' She smiled her thanks at his compliment. 'Mother's feeding you her coffee brew, I see.'

'It's very good.'

'I'm going to leave you two now. I really want to finish off the piece I'm working on.'

'I'd love to see your work. Would you show it to me?'

'That's one of Mum's.' Giles pointed at a small painting on the wall over the back of the solid fuel cooker. 'I love that one. It's a bird that was in the garden one day. I really think she's captured it perfectly.'

'It is nice,' Georgia said from a distance. She rose to look at it more carefully. 'Oh, it's lovely. You're right. She has pictured it perfectly. You're obviously a very good observer. Have you always painted?'

'Oh, yes. I used to draw a lot as a child. I suppose it just grew from that. I'm more into colour, and I paint portraits to keep body and soul together. Come through to my studio, if you want to. Don't feel obliged.'

'No, I'd love to see what you're doing. Thank you.'

It was a large, untidy sort of house, but seemed very cosy and comfortable. She immediately felt at home there. She smiled, thinking how her mother would hate the disorder and chaos every-where. But then, her mother didn't have anything else to do with her time. Mrs Hoburn was obviously very moti-vated to work and didn't mind about having a messy house. At least it seemed like a home, she thought.

'I love your house,' she remarked on her way through to the studio. It was a bright, airy room overlooking the rather messy garden. 'Oh wow,' she said, catching sight of a large painting sitting on the easel. 'That is wonderful.' It was a mass of brilliant blues and greens, obviously a fantasy view of the garden.

'Well, thank you. I haven't finished it yet, of course. I have various colours to be added, to capture the odd few flowers lurking in there.' Georgia looked through the French window. There were a few late spring flowers and several rosebushes almost leaping into bloom. She could really see the whole point of the picture.

'Do you always work in oils?'

'Oh, no. I like to mix my mediums. I shall probably add some pastels at some point. Don't know yet.'

'What else have you done?'

'Oh, I'm sure you don't want to see more. Don't you want to spend time with Giles? He's seen it all before.'

Georgia turned to look at Giles. 'You don't mind, do you?'

'Course not. I keep telling Mum she should be proud of what she's doing.

You look and enjoy. I might go and look at lunch.'

'It's all in the fridge, dear. Just needs putting in the oven.'

'How long will it take to cook?'

'Oh, an hour or two. Not sure, really.'

He sighed, shaking his head. 'I'd better go and put it in, if we plan to eat at all today.'

'Come over here, dear. You can see what else I've been doing lately.' She went to the side of the room where piles of canvases were leaning against a wooden construction. 'Giles put this together for me to store my pictures. Simple but effective.'

'He's very proud of what you do.'

'I'm very proud of him. Didn't do a bad job, considering I raised him on my own.'

'Mrs Hoburn, I really think you're marvellous. Really.'

'Call me Maggie. It's silly for two people to be stuffy, don't you think?'

'Definitely. Thank you . . . Maggie. Now, let me look at your paintings.'

They were an eclectic mix of portraits and other, wilder stuff. She wondered about the woman's ability to paint so carefully in may ways and so madly in others. It showed a sense of discipline which she allowed herself to loosen at times. She clearly had an enormous talent and one which was quite rare.

'Do you have an agent?'

'Not really. I have a friend with a gallery who comes round occasionally and asks me to put on a show for him. But I'm not really interested. I enjoy what I do, and apart from the occasional commission for someone, I pretty well paint what I like.'

'You should put on an exhibition. Let all the world see your talents. Wow, if I had talent like yours, I'd be shouting it from the rooftops.'

'Well, thank you. Here, what do you think of this one?'

She showed her a very peaceful rural scene done in pastels. It looked perfect. One could almost imagine the sheep walking right into the room.

'That's lovely. Quite a change from your usual stuff, though.'

'And this one?' She showed her another oil painting: this one a sea, rough with huge waves, and in the distance a tiny boat being battered by the storm.

'That is lovely. Wow, the waves look as if they might wet your floor any time.'

'Those two are Giles' work. He's also pretty talented.'

'Goodness, I had no idea. He has obviously inherited his ability from you. We don't actually do any painting at Uni, it's all theory, but I do a bit of stuff at home. Nothing on your scale, though. Crumbs, what a talented family. Was your husband an artist too?' She saw a look of pain cross Maggie's features and bit her tongue. 'I'm sorry. I shouldn't have asked.'

'He was gone a long time ago. Yes indeed, he had talent too. He was an architect before he became canon-fodder. He tried not to go, but they decided he was needed. He was a prisoner of war, but he died during his time there.'

'I'm so sorry. I didn't mean to upset you. Giles thought he might have been a teacher.'

'Oh, I'm quite over it all now. I just get frustrated when I think about it. Now, why don't you go and find Giles? He must be thinking I've eaten you or something.'

'Thank you for the tour round your pictures. They are wonderful. Enjoy your work.' She left the room and went back along the corridor to find the kitchen. Giles wasn't there, but there was a wonderful smell of some sort of casserole. She went back into the corridor and called out softly.

'Where are you, Giles?'

'In my room. Come and join me.' He opened his door and she went into his room. It was reasonably clean and tidy, possibly done especially for the occasion. It was a typically male room and very different to her own room at home. In fact, her room was quite devoid of personality, while this screamed *Giles* to her.

'It's lovely,' she said. 'I really like it. In fact, the whole house is very homely. You'd hate our house. It's all well-ordered and immaculate and, I've decided, has no personality. Mummy would hate this, but it's everything anyone could want.'

'You could always come and live here if you wanted to — oh, I'm not suggesting anything, of course. We have an empty room.'

'Seriously? I couldn't afford to pay much rent. But I'd save having a season ticket. What would your mother say?'

'You've met her. She'd be fine about it. I can tell she likes you.'

'She's asked me to call her Maggie.'

'Well, there you are then. Open invitation. Come here, I haven't kissed you today.'

'Yes, you did.'

'That was just a peck of greeting. I mean properly kissed.'

'A peck of greeting. I like that.'

He leaned over to her and kissed her very thoroughly. She responded warmly until they both stopped for breath.

'I'm not sure my moving here would be such a good idea. How on earth would I cope? Knowing you kiss like that.'

'It must be you. I've never kissed anyone before. Apart from various cousins and other friends. But I don't count that.'

'How many cousins do you have?'

'A couple, both girls. Mum's brother's children. We were brought up together when they lived here. They moved away ages ago.'

'Mine all live quite near to us. My grandfather had this wonderful idea of building a massive house that all his family could live in together. My parents moved out when they were first married, and the others moved too before they had children. He's sold it now and lives in a smaller house round the corner from us. He's gone home to our place for Sunday lunch. I was practically ordered to be there, but I said no, I had a date.'

'I'm glad you're here. I'd better go and look at the casserole. It'll be burnt to a crisp otherwise.'

'It smells pretty good. What's in it?'

'I have no idea. Didn't ask. It was pretty amazing it was produced in the first place. I think it's possibly beef-based.'

'Great. I feel quite hungry now.'

'Come on, then. Let's go and examine the oven.'

An hour or so later, they all sat round the kitchen table, having finished the casserole and drunk several glasses of wine.

'No more for me. I have to drive back home at some point.'

'Not for ages yet. But I understand. I'll put some fresh coffee on. Assuming you'd like it?'

'Lovely. Thank you very much. That was a delicious meal.'

'Glad you enjoyed it. At least Giles put it in the oven, or we'd still be waiting. Now, coffee.'

All too soon, it was time she was

leaving. It was already getting dark so she would have to drive home in the twilight. Her parents would worry about her being out in her mother's car, but there was nothing she could do about it now. She almost asked if she might ring to let them know, but decided she would leave it.

'Thank you so much for having me. I've had a lovely day and I love your paintings. Both of you.'

Maggie came close to her and kissed her. 'We've loved having you. Come again soon.'

'Thank you. I will.'

'I suggested she might move into our spare room,' said Giles suddenly. 'I was going to say earlier. Make a lot of sense for Uni. What do you say, Mum?'

'Course she can if she wants to. Any time.'

'That's very good of you. As I said to Giles, I can't pay much in the way of rent. But I can contribute to the food.'

'Think about it, anyway. Now, go and see her off, Giles.'

They went outside to the car.

'Do consider it, won't you?'

'I will. I could always say it's just till Uni finishes. And your mum is lovely. I've had such a good day. Thank you.' She kissed him and got into the car. 'See you tomorrow.'

'Not till later in the day. Our first lecture isn't till two.'

She drove home carefully, arriving a little after nine o'clock. Her parents were waiting in the hall.

'Hallo Mummy, Daddy. I've had a lovely day.'

'Where on earth have you been till now? I thought you were invited for lunch? How could you stay so late? They must have thought you had no manners at all.'

'I'm sorry, I didn't say it was just lunch. We were talking loads. Giles' mother is such an interesting lady. She's a painter. You should see her work, it's truly amazing.'

'I am more concerned with your having outstayed your welcome. It is polite to leave by three at the latest.' Her mother had strange ideas about what was expected and not expected.

'We were still eating at three. I could hardly have left in the middle of the meal, now, could I?'

'Eating at three? What sort of household is that?'

'One that I intend moving into. Maggie has invited me to go and live there. At least until the Uni term is finished.'

'Don't be ridiculous, girl. How on earth can you afford rent?' Her father was full of bluster and was obviously annoyed.

'I'd be there rent-free. I can use the money I save on my season ticket for food. It isn't too far from the Uni, so we could walk there.'

'Never heard such a load of nonsense in my life,' said her father as he went into the sitting room. 'Sort it out, dear. And don't forget to tell her what her grandfather said about her absence.'

'I'm sorry, Mummy. But I do really want to go and live there.'

'It's a silly idea. You can't live in the same house as your boyfriend. Whatever will people say?'

'There is a room I can use. I'm only thinking of a temporary move till the end of term, anyway. It's not all that long.'

'Your grandfather was very upset about your absence.'

'I'm sorry about that, but the order came too late. I didn't want to upset him but I can't help it. I'll call round to see him later in the week. Well, tomorrow perhaps. I can go on my way to the station. I don't have a lecture till the afternoon.'

Her mother looked rather worried. 'I don't like this. Not at all.'

'Night, Mummy. I never meant to give you hassle. And thank you very much for the loan of your car.'

'Night, dear.'

Georgia ran upstairs and went in to see her sister.

'I've had a fabulous day. It was such an amazing place. Huge, though they've sold off a lot of it. And they've offered me a room; rent-free, as well.'

'Goodness. You're not going to take it, though, are you?'

'Oh yes. The parents both objected totally, so that clinched it for me.'

'But is it really . . . well, practical? I mean to say, you've hardly been going out with Giles for more than a few minutes.'

'I know it's the right thing for me to do. It's everything I could ever ask for. And it isn't as if we've only just met. I've known him for almost three years. This time next week, I shall be living in Highgate.'

6

It was Tuesday morning and the day of the Board meeting. George had lain awake for most of the night worrying about it, and about the bombshell dropped by his daughter. How could she make plans like that without consulting her parents? But his immediate problems were how to get his father to see that his plans for the company were going to be beneficial. He had spent most of the previous day writing notes on his pitch, notes which he and his brother Henry had decided on long ago. Now all they had to do was to sell it to their father. Oh, and his sisters, of course. This was the big problem. Six of them on the Board. Always the same problem.

The local caterers had arrived with plates of sandwiches and savouries, and his secretary had laid out cups and saucers. She had also filled the urn, and switched it on for boiling water for tea or coffee. It was the same routine they had followed for many years. Geoffrey had begun it and seemed to expect it to continue in exactly the same way, year in and year out. George went in and laid out duplicate copies of the agenda. They had all been sent them in advance of the meeting, but he knew from experience the two Aunts would have left theirs behind. There was also a notepad for each of them. He had no doubt the Aunts would take theirs with them to use as writing paper.

At midday, he went along to the Boardroom. It was a large room with a big table and six chairs. The food was set out on a side table at one end. He waited for them to arrive. He had placed his own bundle of notes at the head of the table, asserting his position as the senior man. He'd had to fight to get that position, as Geoffrey has previously assumed it. He now sat at the opposite end of the table, so that in effect he was separated from the rest.

'Come on in, Henry. I wanted to talk to you before the others arrive.'

'About the new farms?'

'Yes, and the extension to the shop, of course.'

'The old man doesn't like the idea, I take it?'

'No. He thinks things are moving along nicely as they are. I wondered if there was a way of nobbling one or both of the Aunts. I was going to chat to them while they eat. Do you think you could take on one of them?'

'I can try. But you know how they stick together. Don't hold out a great deal of hope.'

'I thought that if Michael speaks to Father, he might occupy him. Be enthusiastic and try to sell it to them.'

'Okay. Will do. I was actually wondering if we might recruit our wives to the board. Even things up a bit.'

'Now, there's a thought. Maybe something to think about for the future, but there's enough going on today. Here they come. Good luck.'

'Thanks. Good day ladies, Father. Come and help yourselves to food. Do you want tea or coffee?'

'Aunt May. Aunt Janet. How are you both?'

'Fine, thank you dear. Who made the sandwiches?'

'The usual company. Is there anything wrong?'

'Well, I don't care much for the fish ones. There do seem to be rather a lot of those.'

'Come with me and let's see if there are any others you might like.' He shepherded her away from her sister, nudging Henry as he passed him. He immediately went over to Aunt Janet and began to talk to her. Michael had fallen in with his father and seemed to be looking after him very well. So far, so good.

'I trust you have seen our agenda? We're very excited about the shop extension. It really will make such a difference to what we can sell in there.'

'Really, dear? But won't it take up

space you currently use for other things?'

'Oh no, not at all. There's ample room for everything. It really is rather innovative, selling all our products under one roof. We hope to buy in other things, and sell them to our customers too. It will be shopping under one roof, instead of going from shop to shop. Just think, you'll be able to come and buy everything you might want.'

'It does sound a rather good idea.'

'Oh, it is. I trust you'll give us your vote, then?'

'Well, yes. But I will have to see what dear Geoffrey thinks of the idea first.'

'Yes, well, Father is often unable to see the larger picture. He gets a little bogged down with detail.'

'Oh, but he does have a very clear mind for business. You must see that, dear.'

'Oh, of course I respect him. After all, it's down to him that we're all in business at all. That we all get our payouts each year. I suppose I'm thinking of ways to increase all that. It'll mean larger payments for all of us.'

'Oh, I see. I hadn't perhaps realised that. Very well, dear, I shall vote for the new shop.'

'Thank you, Aunt May. Now, if you'll excuse me, I shall go and make sure everyone has eaten what they want. Then we can make a start.'

George felt pleased with his chat and hoped Henry had had equal success. Still, if one of the Aunts voted with the three brothers, it would be enough to carry the motion. Two of them might be even better.

'Ladies and gentlemen, if we could make a start . . . '

He called for his secretary to come in and take the minutes. The company settled down round the table and he began the meeting. The formal part at the beginning was soon dispensed with, though Geoffrey wanted to raise several points from the previous minutes.

'Now we come to the first, most important part of the meeting.' He glanced at May and passed her the ghost of a smile. 'The new shop extension. Henry, Michael and I have given this a great deal of thought and discussion, and we propose taking in a part of the main floor of the dairy and extending the shop so we can sell many more items. It will give much more variety of shopping under one roof.' He continued his description, gave them all his reasons, and then waited. Nobody said a word. Nobody raised any objections. 'Does anyone have an opinion?'

'Good idea,' growled Geoffrey. 'Let's vote on it.'

'Very well. All in favour?' Everyone raised their hands. 'Excellent. Carried unanimously.'

'That was easy,' Michael muttered to his brother.

'Next item is the purchase of two new farms to ensure supplies of milk.' He told them about the two farmers who wanted to sell their farms, and how he had offered them a good purchase price.

'I need to interrupt here,' Geoffrey said loudly. 'It's a ridiculous idea.'

'I'm sorry?' George said. 'In what way ridiculous?'

'Expenditure we can't afford. You don't have that sort of capital to waste. Have you asked yourself why they want to sell? Who will look after the farms? How will milk production be sufficiently increased? Nonsense. Utter nonsense.'

'Can't we at least talk about it?' Henry asked.

'Why waste time?' Geoffrey was taking the lead and had the bit between his teeth.

'I think we need to talk it through, at least.'

'Can't see any point in it.'

'Well perhaps we might have a better idea of what is necessary to further this business,' snapped George, at the end of his tether. 'We desperately need to take on more milk production. Here we have two small farmers wanting to retire and offering us the farms at a decent price. Along with the ones we already own, it will make us almost completely self-sufficient.'

'Almost. *Almost*. There we have the key. You'll still be needing to buy in milk.'

'But it will be a much smaller amount. In time, these two farms will increase production and provide what we need.'

'It is too much money to spend out. You won't have enough in reserve — enough to fall back on. Bankruptcy will be the next step. Then what will happen to all of you? And there are your Aunts to think of. You can't expect them to live in poverty, all as a result of you spending too much money.'

'There probably isn't much point in voting now, but perhaps it could be considered for discussion at the next Board meeting?' Henry was determined it wasn't going to be dismissed.

'No point. These two farmers want a quick sale. If we don't buy them, they'll be auctioned off in the next three weeks. It's now or never.'

'You have my views; and, I'm sure, those of your Aunts.' The two women looked a little sheepish, but nodded together, seeming to have been bullied by their brother.

'Perhaps we three might club together to buy the farms,' suggested Michael, somewhat timorously.

'Now, there's an idea,' agreed Henry.

George stared at his two brothers. It was certainly a suggestion. Geoffrey looked as if he were about to explode.

'We can work out what it will cost us all and see if we can manage it. It will be a cost to the dairy in buying the milk from us directly. I think it could be a good money-spinning idea for all of us. Thank you, Michael.'

'Wait a minute,' Geoffrey intervened. 'How can you possibly afford to buy two farms yourselves?'

'Oh, bank loans; and I can certainly raise a few thousand.' George knew it might be a struggle for him, but felt determined to get his wishes agreed one way or another.

'This is ridiculous,' the old man told them, sitting back with his arms folded.

'You're using that word rather a lot. I think this is something my brothers and I should discuss. It's no longer a Board matter. Not if we're taking it out of the dairy itself. Now, if we can move on. Any other business?'

The two Aunts looked most uncomfortable and shook their heads. He looked at his brothers, who both shook their heads.

'Father?'

'I don't like this. Not at all. Why do you want these two farms so badly?'

'To provide the extra milk we need, to keep up with demand. The last quarter shows a huge rise in profits, so it seems logical to use this to buy more supplies. But you and the Aunts don't want it, so we have to find an alternative. Michael has come up with a solution.'

'I'll think about it. Give me the figures to back up your ideas, and I'll consider it carefully. What with the costs of extending the shop and everything else, I doubt you'll afford another purchase like this one.'

'We don't actually have much time. I said we'd give them an answer tomorrow.'

'I'll look this evening. I assume you have the figures?'

'Of course.' George shuffled among his pile of papers and handed over a list of figures and written sheets which he'd been using to make his plea. 'I shall want it back. It's the only detailed copy. Right, well, I say we call it a day. Thank you all for attending and giving of your time so generously.'

'Don't mention it, dear,' said Aunt May. 'Always a pleasure to visit the dairy. Now, what is going to happen to the leftover food? I'll wrap it and take it with me. Make a nice addition to supper. If nobody else wants it of course?' They shook their heads. It was more than their lives were worth to deprive the Aunts of the leftover sandwiches. May bustled over to the table and began to pack them up. Aunt Janet collected several of the notepads and stuffed them into her capacious handbag.

'Don't like waste, dear,' she muttered.

'Are you going to drive us home, dear?' May asked her brother.

'One of the boys will take you. I'm going to look at George's figures now.' He was dismissive of them now the business of the day was over.

'I suppose it's down to me,' said Michael resignedly. 'Come on then.'

'Thank you, dear. Bye-bye now. Interesting meeting, George, Henry.'

They left the room behind their nephew and spoke to several of the workers on their way through.

'Where are James and Phillip working? I'd like to see them.'

'I'm afraid we don't really have time now, Aunt May. I still have work to do and need to get back.'

'Oh, I'm sorry to inconvenience you.'

'Not at all. I'm pleased to drive you home,' he told them. 'Only, if we don't get along soon, it will be the end of the day and I won't ever get finished.' He scurried them out to his car and shut the door, cursing their garrulousness now they were out of the meeting.

'Now, how is dear Victoria?'

'My wife is fine, thank you. As are our sons.'

'It's a long time since we've seen them.'

'I'll get Victoria to invite you over soon.'

'Oh, thank you dear. We're free on Sunday. Around midday?'

'I'll have to check. Victoria will ring you with a date.'

'I'll make a note in my diary when we get home.'

Michael cursed silently. He knew his wife would hate the idea. She was younger than him and did rather despise the hold the Aunts had over them all. They chatted all the way, rarely giving him time to answer their interrogation.

'I'll give you the key, dear. Perhaps you can open the door for us. Check there aren't any burglars inside,' laughed Janet.

'I don't suppose there will be. But all right.' He took the key and went to open the door. He hated the smell that seemed to linger round their home. It seemed like an old-people smell, masked with judicious quantities of lavender water. It was a smell he would always associate with his Aunts. 'Well, goodbye now. I'll get Victoria to ring you.'

'Thank you, dear. It will be lovely to see your little family.'

He got back into his car and drove to the dairy. There were several people waiting for him, so he was soon back into the swing of everything.

In the boardroom, Geoffrey was studying the plans for buying the two farms. George had returned to his office and Henry was back in his domain. The old man had to admit, the proposal did make a lot of sense. How could he now back down from his previous statement without losing face? He rose and went into George's office.

'What do you think?'

'If you really want to go ahead with it, then do so. It is a stupid idea, but if you're willing to back it with your own money, then I will raise no objections if you decide to use the dairy's finances.'

'Well, thank you, Father. I'm glad you can see the benefits. It will make a huge difference to our turnover. I'll call them both in for a meeting tomorrow. They'll be pleased.'

'What time?'

'Sorry?'

'What time will your meeting be? Only I'd better be here. Make sure you get a good deal.'

'Ten o'clock. Then we'll see you at ten.'

'I'll tell the others to clear their morning. You don't want the Aunts to be here too, I assume?'

'I don't think they have anything to contribute, do you?'

'Not at all. Fine. See you tomorrow.'

George did a little dance of triumph when his father left. He called his brothers back to tell them the news, and then went home.

'You're early,' Nicola said.

'A bitch of a meeting. But he came

round in the end. He's agreed to us buying the farms and to the shop extension. So, all in all, a good outcome. What's new with you?'

'Absolutely nothing. Mrs Henders turned up as usual. Complained about her bunions. So what happens next?'

'Meeting tomorrow with the two farmers. Father insists on being there, but he has agreed to it, so he's coming to meet the farmers. We now have to think about who will manage it.'

'I suppose that means you'll be interviewing again. How nice.'

'I suppose so. I just hope Father doesn't want to be there for that. He'll hate anyone who applies. This will give us a total of twelve farms in our possession. I'm really looking forward to it.'

7

While her father was engaged in his Board meeting, Georgia was discussing her future with Giles. She told him she wanted to move into their spare room as soon as possible.

'That's terrific. You can come whenever you like. You must realise, however, that life in our household is not very organised. Mum's often painting and there's no meal ready, ever. I often have to cook.'

'It sounds wonderful. Mind you, I have no idea about cooking. Maybe I can open beans and make toast.'

He laughed. 'I have an aversion to beans on toast. You'll soon learn. When will you come?'

'I could bring some stuff with me tomorrow, if that's not too soon. I'll bring all my basic stuff and a few clothes. I can maybe go back and get more at the weekend.'

'Great. I'll tell Mum this evening. Then I'll probably have to clean your room, and clear some stuff out of it. What will your parents say?'

'Oh, they'll undoubtedly rant and rave at me. But I shall ignore them. In fact, I probably won't tell them till tomorrow. Oh, I can't wait. It'll be brilliant.'

'It'll be brilliant for me to have you so much closer. Oh, Georgia, I can't imagine how I'll feel having you in the next room.'

'Having breakfast together each day. Travelling to Uni together. Lucky we're doing the same course, isn't it? We can do everything together.'

She didn't notice Giles' face change slightly. He smiled at her enthusiasm, but suddenly he was realising the changes she was going to bring to his easy-going lifestyle. He adored his mother and her work. He loved to spend time in the same room as her, working on his own painting. That was all going to change. Would she allow him his own space?

Would he be able to continue to work alongside his mother? Somehow, he doubted it. He smiled at her.

'I'm glad you're so enthusiastic. It will be such a change for you. For all of us, I guess. Look, I'm going to get home now. Prepare for your arrival tomorrow.'

'You're sure your mum will be okay with all of this? I mean, it will make a difference to the way your home runs.'

'She'll cope. She always does.'

'Okay then. I'll be over in the morning. I'll bring my suitcase to your place before Uni. I don't think we have anything early tomorrow, do we?'

'Well, yes, I have a tutorial first thing. Bring your case into college; you can store it in the bursar's office. She won't mind, I'm sure.'

'Oh, all right then, I will. I won't actually be that early. I'll have to face my parents' wrath. But if I'm going, I'm going. There isn't much they can do about it, is there?'

'I don't want you to anger them so much they won't see you any more.'

'They'll get over it. I told them I was moving out soon. It's just a bit earlier than they're expecting. Go on, then. Go home and prepare for your new lodger.' She leaned over and kissed him. He left her standing there, and wondered what he'd done. He certainly felt more for this girl . . . woman . . . than he'd ever felt for anyone else. He walked back to his home, taking far longer than he would have done if he'd gone by bus.

'I'm home,' he called out. 'Are you busy, Mum?'

'Come on in. I'm just finishing something.' He went into her studio.

'That's great, Mum. Really great.'

'I am quite pleased with it. Once it's dry, I shall varnish it, and then off it goes. I hope they like it.'

'Couldn't help themselves. Mum. You remember offering Georgia the spare room?' She nodded. 'She'd like to move in.'

'Terrific. You'll be pleased with that. When does she want to come?'

'Tomorrow.'

'Oh. A bit soon, isn't it?'

'Well, she's not happy at home. I think this is her way of dealing with it. I've said it will be okay. I'll go and clear out the rubbish we've dumped in there. And put some clean sheets on the bed. Assuming there *are* some clean sheets.'

'You know, Giles, I have no idea. I'll be done soon. I'll come and help.'

'Okay. Thanks.' He went into the spare room and sighed. It was total chaos. He couldn't even see the bed, let alone see if there were clean sheets on it. He began to look at the stuff that was piled up. A lot of it was rubbish that could go straight into the dustbin. As for the rest, he simply had no idea of what he would do with it. He piled it up in the passageway and set about cleaning the room. The bed did not have clean sheets, and nor were there any in the cupboard.

'I think we'll have to buy some more, Mum. The duvet's pretty past it too.'

'Oh, heavens. What on earth can we do?'

'Can't you go and get some tomorrow morning? I've got a tutorial first thing.'

'I suppose I'll have to. You can't put her off for a day or two?'

'Not really. I suppose I could phone her at home, but I don't really want to. It would be rather tricky.'

'I suppose so. I'll just have to go shopping, then. Anything else we'll need?'

'Towels, I guess.'

'Make a list for me. I'll be pretty short of time.'

Giles sat down and made a list. He hoped to goodness his mother would manage to get everything. He usually went with her to buy such things, but there was nothing he could do about it now, except keep his fingers crossed.

Feeling very excited about her plans, Georgia arrived home and went straight up to her room. She opened her rather extensive wardrobe and began to check what she would take with her. She would have to carry everything on the train, so needed to limit what she took.

She decided to sort out her make-up first. That would take up a lot of room, but she must have it all. And her lotions, and stuff to keep her hair nice . . .

The pile was growing. She looked at her bag: she'd almost filled it with what she'd put out. There was little room for clothes. Perhaps she'd better think again. She put half her make-up and lotions back in her bathroom. That left some space for clothes. Not a huge amount, but she could still pack a few different outfits. She thought about the old-fashioned serving girls who seemed to pack everything in a carpet-bag, and shook her head. She heard Maria come to her door, tap on it and come in.

'What on earth are you doing?' she said, in a voice loud enough to be heard by Giles in Highgate.

'Ssh. I'm packing.'

'But why?'

'I'm moving in with Giles and his mother. I mentioned it before. Well, it's happening. I'm going tomorrow.'

'But you can't go. I shall miss you.'

'You'll soon get used to it. I'll be back soon to collect some more stuff.'

'How can you be so cold about it?'

'I'm not. But I'm not telling the parents till tomorrow. So don't you let on, please.'

'I don't know how you can be so calm about this.'

'Age, my dear child. Don't forget I'm a lot older than you. And I'm moving to live with a very special person in my life.'

'Is he so very special?'

'Yes. He's gorgeous. Everything I could want. Not that the parents would approve. His mother's somewhat scatty. She's a painter, as I said, and lives a bit hand-to-mouth.'

'I reckon Daddy will cancel all your payments. He'll ask why he should pay for you to live somewhere else. And it's going to be your twenty-first soon. Are you willing to jeopardise that?'

'What, a ghastly meal with the cousins and their families? Maybe they'll give me the money instead.'

'You'll be lucky. I think they'll freak out and simply decide to ignore the occasion.'

'So be it. I'll just have to get a job; work in Woollies or something.'

'When will you have time?'

'Saturdays, I guess. Oh, I don't know. I can cash in my season ticket and walk to most places. That'll keep me going for a bit.'

'I give up. I'm going to do my homework.'

'You're a very good girl. Maria, you do know it isn't you, don't you? I'm really wanting to live in Town. Where Giles and his Mum live isn't too far from the university.'

'It's the way you're sneaking off they'll hate. But it's up to you.' She left the room, banging the door as she went. Georgia sighed. She really needed an ally here, and it looked as if she'd just lost her chance of keeping her sister on-side.

She finished her packing, having decided to leave most of her make-up and things behind. She had put what she considered her essentials into her handbag, and this was now very full indeed. She had managed to cram in several different outfits, though they would need ironing when she unpacked them. She rather wished she'd seen the room she'd be using. How much wardrobe space would she have, and how many drawers? She'd undoubtedly share the bathroom with both of them. It would be quite a change from her own en-suite here. She glanced at her pretty room and spacious wardrobe, and worried that she might miss it all. Instead, she might have a small room with just a bed in it. Thinking about the rest of the house where Giles lived, it had rather old-fashioned furniture; and, well, it was pretty untidy. Was she making a huge mistake? It was maybe rather soon in their relationship. After all, she'd only gone there last Sunday for the first time. She heard her mother calling her for dinner, and shut her bag away in the wardrobe.

'Had a nice day, dear?' asked Nicola.

'Not bad. You?'

'The usual. Your father had a much more exciting time. A Board meeting.'

'Oh, dear. Is he in a good mood or a bad one?'

'Very good. He got his way over a couple of major projects so he's feeling very happy.'

'That's good. I'm pleased for him. Where is he, by the way?'

'He's talking to Henry on the phone. Making plans for tomorrow, I understand. He's talking about taking us out for dinner tomorrow night. Maybe going into Town. What do you think of that?'

'I, er . . . I'm not sure. I have a late lecture,' she improvised.

'Really? Well, maybe we could meet you in Town. You're bound to finish by seven o'clock, aren't you?'

'I'm not sure. You'd better leave me out of your plans.'

Her father came in at this point and kissed them all.

'Congratulate your clever father,

girls. We are about to expand the dairy. We're going to buy two more farms and extend the shop. How about that?'

'Well done, Daddy. I'm sure you'll be very successful. Don't you think so Georgia?'

'Yes, indeed. Well done.' She was rather lacking in enthusiasm, but hopefully he hadn't noticed.

'I'm going to take us all out for dinner tomorrow night. How about Wheeler's? I'll phone and book a table. Now, shall I open a bottle of wine? Red or white?'

'White would be more suitable. I'll bring in the food right away.' Nicola smiled happily at her family. With George in such a good mood, and her two daughters, she began to feel as if all was well in her world.

Georgia was steadily feeling more and more uncomfortable. Maria kept asking her to agree with them, and she didn't want to, because she wouldn't be there. She knew she was being particularly devious, and it upset her terribly.

After her earlier doubts about her decision, it had not come at a good time. Naturally, she was pleased for her father that things were going well, but she could say little. At last, with pudding more or less finished, she excused herself, claiming she had work to do.

'Well, make sure you don't have anything pressing tomorrow. I intend to celebrate and I want my favourite people there with me.'

She smiled and said goodnight. She went up to her room for what might actually be the last time. Perhaps she should delay her move for another day. She could phone Giles and tell him something had come up. But was that fair? He must have spent the evening clearing out her room, and was probably feeling exhausted. If only she had known it might have been by far the best thing she could have done. She heard her parents go into their room and went downstairs. She picked up the telephone, and put it down again. If she didn't go tomorrow, she might be persuaded out of her plans forever. She crept back up to her room and quietly closed the door. It was opened seconds later by Maria.

'What are you doing? I heard you go downstairs.'

'I was going to call Giles, but decided it might be too late.'

'Why? You'll be seeing him tomorrow.'

'Oh, it's nothing. I wanted to check up on wardrobe space. Go on. Off to bed with you.'

'Can't I creep in with you? Just for a bit.'

'Oh, come on, then.'

The two sisters lay side by side chatting about inconsequential things: remembering holidays and suchlike. They got the giggles at one point, and each tried to quieten the other down — which made them giggle even more.

'We don't want to wake the parents. You should go back to your room now. You'll be worn out tomorrow.'

'I'm all warm and cosy here. Let's just go to sleep.'

'Okay. We'll try.' They both lay quietly and soon fell asleep. Georgia felt comforted by having her sister there, and forgot about the trauma she was about to cause. It would have been so much easier to stay here.

Next morning, determined, she grimaced. Once she was dressed, she picked up her bags and went downstairs.

'Why are you taking that to Uni?' asked her mother.

'I'm moving in with Giles and his mother. I've arranged to go today.'

'But your father's booked a meal for us all tonight.'

'I know. I'm sorry.'

'You might have said something before he booked it. How very inconvenient of you.'

'Mummy. I'm moving out. I won't be living here any more. Don't you understand?'

'Nonsense, dear. You won't stick it for

more than a couple of days. You'll be back with your tail between your legs. Go tomorrow if you really must. He'll be furious if you miss out on tonight. It's the first time in ages he's asked us all to go to together.'

'I don't understand you, Mummy. I really am going. Today. I can't carry everything, so I'll be back soon to collect more of my stuff.'

'Well, you can tell your father.'

'Where is he?'

'He's already gone to the dairy. Some meeting with his brothers.'

'Well, I'm sorry, I won't be here tonight.'

'Really, you are most ungrateful. And what about your sister? What on earth is she going to think?'

'She'll cope. Just as she always does.'

'Where is she anyway?'

'Dunno. Getting ready, I expect. I must collect my stuff and get on my way.'

'Georgia, you can't go. Not like this. Please. At least wait to say goodbye to

Maria.' Nicola felt desperate and was ready to try anything to stop her from going. 'What about money? Daddy is hardly likely to keep paying you an allowance.'

'I'll have to get a job, then.'

'But how can you? Where will you possibly work?'

'There's always Woollies. I said that to Maria.'

'You mean she knows about your crazy plan?'

'Only since last night.'

'Before we had dinner?'

'Well, yes.'

'How could she? How could she keep it from us like that? Maria! Come down here at once.' They heard her coming noisily down the stairs.

'What's the matter?' Her school tie was hanging round her neck and she was obviously in the process of dressing.

'You knew about your sister's plan to leave home?'

Maria looked at her sister, who nodded.

'Well, yes. She told us on Sunday she was going to leave.'

'But did you know she was planning to go today?'

'I only knew last night.'

'How could you? How could you not tell us?'

'Because Georgia asked me not to.'

'Where's your loyalty?'

'I'll be late for school if I don't go now. I'm sorry, okay?' She went back upstairs and the two women were left alone again.

'I'd better go now. Bye, Mummy. I'll call you soon.'

'Please, Georgia. Please don't go. Not like this.'

'Sorry, Mummy. I love you.' She leaned over to kiss her mother, but Nicola turned away.

Georgia shrugged, picked up her bags and left the house. It seemed a long walk to the station, carrying her large heavy load. Even her shoulder-bag seemed to weigh a ton today. Maybe she needed to think about make-up in future. She wondered what Giles thought of it. She also wondered about how much work Giles had done to get ready for her. She was under no illusions about his mother helping him; Maggie would have far too many other things to be doing than get rooms ready. She thought about sheets and towels. Maybe she should have brought some — but then, she could never have carried them along with her clothes. At last she reached the station, and found a seat on the crowded train. The last time she needed to make this journey; for a while, anyway.

When she reached the university campus, she went to the office.

'Could I possibly leave my bag here for today?'

'I'm sorry, dear; not really. You could try the porter's office. He might let you.'

'Okay, thanks. Along here, isn't it?'

'That's right.'

She walked along the passage and came to a small room. She knocked at the door and asked if she might leave her bag there until the end of the day.

'Go on then, miss. Not a lot of room, but it'll be all right.' She thanked him and left it on his none-too-clean floor. She went in search of Giles. She longed to see him and feel his comforting hugs. He was in a tutorial, and probably wouldn't be out of it till almost lunchtime.

She went into the library and tried to settle down to some reading, but her concentration had disappeared completely. By lunchtime, she felt somewhat desperate to see him, and sat in the canteen. At last he came in, and waved at her as he went to join the queue. He came and sat by her.

'So, how did it go?' he asked.

'Daddy was already at the dairy so it was just Mummy. She was not very pleased. Her main concern seemed to be that I was letting them down for a family dinner tonight. They're going to Wheeler's, and he'd booked it and everything. Still, they can go without me, can't they? How about you? How did the big clear-out go?'

'Well,' he said slowly, 'not all that well. There's still loads of stuff lurking there, but at least it's now piled together in one corner. We'll gradually get rid of it. I'm just hoping Mum will manage to do the rest.'

'The rest?'

'One or two things we needed. She promised to go shopping, but no doubt she'll get absorbed in something and forget.'

'I'm sorry to give you so much trouble.'

'Nonsense. It needed something to make me do it. Now, who have we got this afternoon?'

'Can't remember. It's in the lecture theatre, anyway. How was your tutorial, by the way?'

'Fine. He's a good bloke.' They chatted about various lecturers as they walked along. They reached the lecture theatre and went inside, sitting with a lot of others, awaiting their lecturer. It was a woman who didn't really have a great deal new to tell them, but they all politely listened. She finished and they all left the lecture room.

'Could have done without that one,' grumbled Georgia. 'I think your Mum would have been a lot more interesting.'

'Now, there's a thought,' laughed Giles. 'Mrs Hoburn will speak today on Making-Do and Mending . . . '

'Fool. She really would have done something interesting, though. Hasn't she ever considered it?'

'What, my Mum? No. Why would she?'

'I don't know. She's interesting, and I think she'd talk really well. Oh, it's just my way of thinking. If we're done here, shall we go home?'

'Can't see why not. Have you got a bag of some sort?'

'In the porter's room.'

They collected her bag and set off to her new home. It was about a mile to walk, so they decided to take a bus. Giles was worried about arriving home

— as he usually did — to find his mother ensconced in her studio, painting as if her world depended on it. All was quiet and he called out. There was no response.

'She must have gone out somewhere,' he said. 'I'll put the kettle on. I'm sure you could do with a cuppa.' He put the kettle on and left her sitting in the kitchen. He went along to her room and checked to see if there were sheets on the bed. There were, and two towels were laid out. He breathed a sigh of relief. His mother could come up with the goods occasionally. He glanced into her studio, but it was empty.

'I've made some tea. Hope that was okay.'

'Course. It's your home now, so you must feel free to help yourself to anything you want.'

'Thanks. It'll take me a while to find out where everything is stored.'

'There's not a lot of stuff stored anywhere. We're a bit hand-to-mouth. Not very organised, I'm afraid. I often cook our evening meal.'

'Really? Goodness me, a man who can cook. I doubt my father could even find his way to put the grill on to make toast.'

'Well, feel free to cook whenever you want to.'

'Me? I'm afraid I can't cook at all. I did tell you I couldn't. My mother would never let me into her kitchen apart from carrying the dirty dishes through. Must admit, I rarely ever did that either.'

He looked at her curiously.

'You're going to find things rather different here. Mum sometimes doesn't come out of her studio till quite late. If I didn't cook something, I doubt she'd even eat. I'm not a brilliant cook, by the way, so don't expect anything too exotic.'

'It'll be nice to have some good plain food. My mother is always experimenting with recipes from her latest cookery book. Some of them can be almost edible.' They finished drinking their tea and he led her along to her room. As she expected, it was fairly basic, with not a great deal of storage space. She would have to limit what she brought from home, but it wouldn't really be a problem.

'I'll leave you to unpack. There is some drawer space, and . . . well, hooks to hang things on. I hope that will do for you.'

'It'll be fine. Thank you.' She reached for him and he gave her a hug. It turned into a long kiss. They heard Maggie come in. She called out,

'Are you home yet? I've brought fish and chips for supper. Thought we'd have us a treat.'

Georgia smiled and they went out to the kitchen to join her. Fish and chips? As a treat? She hadn't eaten anything like that for ages.

8

At ten o'clock that morning precisely, George was sitting in the boardroom, awaiting his brothers and father. The two farmers were arriving separately and he wanted everything ready for them to sign. The rest of the party came in, and he called them all to order.

'I have the transfer documents here ready for them to sign. I'll get them sent to our solicitors with the signatures of the two farmers. Any questions?'

'Have they agreed to the price?'

'Oh yes, of course. It's included in the documents.'

'And how soon will they move out?'

'On completion of the sales. We really need to get a move on to find someone to manage them. I've drafted out an advert to put in the *Farmers Weekly*. I thought I'd put it in the local press, too.'

They all agreed; and, despite his concerns, their father remained quiet throughout. The first farmer arrived, looking rather nervous. He was twisting his cap in his hands as he came into the Boardroom. George did his best to put him at his ease, and soon the document was signed and he was being shown out. The second farmer arrived a little later, and seemed quite a different prospect.

'I've bin thinking, like,' he began. 'I don't have anywhere to go and live when the time comes. I wondered if you'd want to employ me, like, to manage the farm for you? I can keep it going all right. With a bit more cash, I can make it profitable. What do you say?'

'Well,' George replied, the wind slightly taken out of his sails, 'we shall have to discuss that between ourselves. Perhaps you'd be good enough to step out of the room for a few minutes.' The farmer got up and left the room.

'Looks like a reasonable idea to me,'

said Michael. 'He knows the farm pretty well and we're looking for someone to manage it anyway.'

'I don't like the idea at all,' Henry put in. 'Why would he want to carry on living there, if it wasn't his?'

'I agree with Henry,' their father told them. 'It's a bit too close to him to move on. What is it, twenty-five acres? Not enough to make a lot of profit, but about enough for a herd of cows. I don't think he'll be much use.'

'Okay. Sorry, Michael. Can you fetch him back?'

The farmer stood before them, looking fairly confident.

'I'm afraid it's no. We feel it's important for us to appoint a new person. We shall want to re-organise things somewhat.'

'I can do that, sir. I'd be happy to work however you wanted me to. I suppose you'd want more cows and more milk. I can do that for you.'

'I'm sorry,' said George. 'We've made our decision. I'm sure you'll soon find somewhere else to live. With money behind you, you'll find another business.'

'But you don't understand. I'm on me own now. My missus passed on recently, and I've got several kids to feed. I need somewhere for us to live together.'

'Let's get the documents signed. We'll give it more thought, I promise you. I'll let you know soon.'

'I suppose that'll have to do. Where do I sign?'

George handed him the document and he signed in a faltering hand.

'Don't you want to read it first?'

'Nah, I'm sure I can trust you. Thank you, sirs. I'll hope to hear summat from you soon.' He left them and they looked at each other.

'We did get quite a bargain, you know,' began Michael.

'He did sound rather pathetic. Perhaps we should reconsider.'

'I don't think that's any reason to employ him — because we feel sorry for him.'

'I think he'd work fairly hard to make himself worthwhile. But it's up to all of you.'

'I'll give it some thought,' promised George. 'I think that concludes the business for today. Anyone disagree?'

They all muttered, and gradually left the room.

'That was all quite satisfactory, don't you think, my boy?' Geoffrey was rather pompous. He got up to leave. 'You sorted out your girl yet?'

'Georgia, you mean? Not really.'

'Disappointing. I wanted to see her. Her twenty-first soon. I wanted to discuss what she'd like as a gift. Make sure she's around next time I call.'

'I'll try, but she's got a will of her own.'

'I'm wondering if I might transfer a portion of shares to her. Just a small amount, so she's more involved in what we're doing. I plan to do the same for the others when their time comes. They won't have any voting rights, of course.'

'That's very generous of you, Father.

It sounds like a good idea to me.'

'Right. Well, I'll decide when I've had a chance to speak to her.'

'Can I mention it to her?'

'I can't see why not.'

'I'm taking us all out for dinner this evening. Wheeler's. I might mention it then.'

'Don't make it a firm promise. Just say I'm thinking about it.'

'Very well, Father. I'll say thank you on her behalf. Now, if you'll excuse me, I must get on.'

'I'll have a walk round and then I'll go home to my lonely lunch.'

The day wore on until George decided he'd done enough, packed his briefcase and went home. He called out to his wife when he arrived.

'What time are we meeting Georgia?' he asked.

'Oh, George,' she burst out. 'The wretched girl has gone.'

'What do you mean, gone? Where has she gone?'

'To live with that boy. I don't

understand it at all. We've given her everything she could possibly want.'

'Damnation. Father wants to see her before her twenty-first. He intends giving her some shares. What on earth do I tell him now?'

'Aren't you concerned for her? She's living with some boy we haven't even met. I don't even have a phone number for her. How do I get in touch with her?'

'Have you asked Maria? She'll probably know where she is.'

'She says not. I don't know whether to believe her or not.'

'I'll get the truth out of her. Maria! Come down here immediately.'

'She's doing her homework so she's ready to go out.'

'What's up?' said Maria as she came downstairs.

'What do you think is up? Where's your sister gone?'

'I don't know. Highgate, somewhere. She's gone to live with Giles and his mother.'

'His mother? She lives there too? She condones these sort of goings-on?'

'I don't think they're actually living together. Well, not the way you mean it. She said they've got a spare room.'

'That's something, I suppose. Are you sure she didn't tell you her phone number?'

'Not at all, I have no idea about it. She said she'd be coming back to fetch some more of her things soon. Perhaps you can ask her then. Now, are we still going out or not? If we are, then I need to finish off my essay.'

'I don't see how we can have a family celebration. What on earth is there to celebrate?' moaned Nicola.

'I'd better call Wheeler's and cancel our table. Damn the girl. Typical of her to cause so much trouble. Is there anything to eat? Can you provide us with dinner?'

'I suppose so. Nothing very special, though. I'd better go and make a start. Really, it is so inconvenient. How could she do this to me?'

'To all of us,' added Maria sadly.

'I'll be in my study,' George told them, disappearing though the door.

It was a gloomy trio who sat down to omelette and chips. George complained bitterly about the quality of the meal.

'Not quite up to Wheeler's standards,' he moaned.

'Of course it isn't, I wasn't expecting to have to cook anything tonight. It's a good job I had some eggs in the fridge. I don't know what we'd have done without them.'

'The farm sale went off all right,' he said at last. 'We now own two more farms. Should make a difference to our milk production. I'm also thinking we should open a couple more shops. There are one or two around London, but more would bring in more profit.' He went on about dairy-related matters, while Nicola thought of the difference Georgia's absence would make to her life. Another year and a half, and Maria would also be going away. She thought about endless dinners with just the two of them sitting across from each other. She wondered what on earth they would ever talk about. It was sometimes difficult enough to talk with the family around them. She wondered if the others felt as she did: Henry and Sophie, Michael and Victoria . . . She got on best with Victoria.

'So, what do you think?' asked George.

'I'm sorry, I was miles away. What did you ask me?'

'Would you have employed the farmer who was leaving to manage his farm for us?'

'Oh yes, I'd have thought he'd be the best person you could employ. He knows his farm probably better than anyone else could. Has he got a wife?'

'She's dead. He's got what he called *several children*.'

'Maybe one of them will stay on to look after the rest.'

'Maybe. I'm inclined to give him a go. Michael was all in favour; Henry was dead against. Father was somewhere in-between.'

'So, do you want some fruit? I haven't had time to make a pudding.'

'Some cheese and biscuits might suit me better. A bit of a lightish meal.'

'Well, I'm sorry; I didn't exactly have much time, did I? I did the best I could manage.'

'I don't know how long these things take.'

'I'll go and get some cheese. What about you, Maria? Do you want cheese or fruit?'

'Yes, please.'

'Well, which?'

'I'll have both, please. Dad's right. It was a bit sparse actually.'

Nicola scowled and went into the kitchen. Honestly, what did they expect? She had been expecting a lavish meal at a posh London restaurant too. Georgia had done her out of that. She obviously didn't care about the rest of the family. How could she go like that? Nicola asked herself for the umpteenth time that day. She plonked cheese on the board, added a couple of apples, picked up some plates and took it all into the dining room.

'Mm, I enjoyed that,' Maria said. 'We should have it more often. Can I have another cracker, please?' She ate with relish, wiping her mouth on the back of her hand.

'Really, Maria; use your napkin. Haven't you any manners?'

'Sorry,' she replied meekly. 'May I leave the table?'

'Of course, dear.'

'Do you want me to help clear? Only I've still got some homework to finish.'

'Help your mother first.'

She sighed at her father's words. 'I wondered if you might help, actually.'

'Me? Don't be ridiculous,' he snapped

'It's all right, I'll manage; there aren't many dishes. You go and finish your homework.' Her mother tried to be conciliatory to the girl. They both wanted her to succeed in her A-levels, and one washing-up session missed was hardly going to matter.

Maria ran upstairs and shut herself in her room. She sat staring at her books laid out on her desk, and sighed. She was really missing her sister being in the next room. She doodled for a while and then went to lie on her bed. She felt no guilt whatsoever about missing out on helping with the dishes, even if she wasn't doing her homework. She had nothing pressing, having really cleared her evening to go out.

Nicola did the washing-up with bad grace. Why had her husband said it was ridiculous for him to help out? He was inherently lazy, she decided. He paid for her daily helper and assumed she didn't need any more support. Oh no, of course not. He was much too important in his dairy. She sometimes wondered about that dairy. Why couldn't they simply retire and move to Cornwall? She adored Cornwall and would love to live there. But he was much too young to retire. Knowing him, it would be many years yet before he was willing even to consider it. Though she was only in her fifties, she felt so bored with her life that retirement seemed a very nice prospect.

In his study, George sat staring into space. He felt irritated beyond words about his elder daughter, and wondered what to do to bring her back into line. Perhaps if he held back her allowance, that might do it. He made a note to remind himself to cancel the standing order at the bank the next day. Damn the girl. He wanted her here at home where he could keep his eye on her and make sure she was actually working. He thought about her, and did actually wonder if he really had any idea of her progress through University. She had mentioned some boyfriend or other, and yet hadn't brought him home. Could she be afraid of us not liking him? he wondered. Surely she should be proud of their home — and they were fine parents, weren't they? And then there was his father's offer to make some shares over to her for her twenty-first. What on earth was he going to think when told she had left home? He shook his head in despair and picked up the daily paper. He went to join his wife later when she was watching the television.

'What's on?' he asked.

'Oh, just some quiz show. I'm only watching to alleviate my boredom. There's a nature programme on after this. Might be interesting.'

'I might go down to the club and see if anyone's around for a game of snooker. I'll see you later.'

'You go and enjoy yourself,' she said, with a hugely sarcastic emphasis on each word. 'I'll just sit here.'

'Jolly good. I'll see you later.'

'So you said. I'll try not to die of boredom in the meantime.' This, she said after he had left the room, so he didn't hear it; or if he did, he made no comment. She really had to do something. Many people would have envied her lifestyle: help in the house to do the cleaning; two grown-up, or nearly so, daughters, both doing well; a well-to-do husband who would always bring things home from the dairy and shop. She had nothing to complain about, really.

Except that she had too little to do. She had been brought up in times when education for women was really only available for someone who was brilliant and wanted to succeed. She had learned about cookery to some extent, and had been on the odd lampshade-making course. She had tried dressmaking too, but never felt very pleased with the results. Besides, she had no real need to do it: she could easily afford to buy whatever clothes she wanted. Nicola sighed and sat back to watch the nature programme, no further on with her resolution to find a new interest in life.

By the time George returned, infinitely happier than when he left thanks to a few drinks, his wife was already in bed. He spoke to her but she didn't respond. He assumed she must be asleep or feigning it to avoid further conversation. He got ready and crept in beside her. He wriggled to make himself comfortable and fell into a deep sleep. He began to snore, and in despair, Nicola got out of bed and went into Georgia's room. She climbed into her daughter's bed and tried to sleep. At least the sheets were clean, she thought, as she drifted off.

The next morning, she awoke wondering where on earth she was. She went into her own room and found George was still asleep. Noisily, she went into their bathroom and washed and dressed.

'Wake up. You'll be late for the dairy.'

'Wassup?' he mumbled, coming out of his deep slumbers. 'Oh, it's you. I'm awake now. I'll be down soon. Bacon for breakfast? With a few mushrooms would be nice.'

'And where am I supposed to get mushrooms at this hour of the day?'

'Haven't you got some? Oh, well, tomatoes will do then. And a fried slice of bread to bulk it out a bit.' He lay back, looking forward to his breakfast.

Angrily, Nicola went downstairs. She was nothing more than someone to cook his meals and sort his washing. He could have a housekeeper to do that for him. She felt tempted to go away for a few days and leave them to cope on their own, but knew she couldn't do that, for Maria's sake. She realised she hadn't woken her daughter and went to call her. Why did everyone rely on her all the time? They didn't take responsibility for their own actions. Was it her fault? Had she always spoiled them? Possibly. With a sigh, she reached for the frying pan and put several slices of bacon into it.

'I was thinking about what you said last night,' George said, coming into the kitchen. 'About the farmer looking after his farm after we've bought it. Makes sense. I think I'll persuade the others it's a good idea.'

'Good.'

'I'll call them all together this morning and we can write to the chap. Is my breakfast ready?'

'The tea's on the table; pour some for yourself,' she snapped. 'The bacon won't be long.'

'Is Maria gracing us with her presence? Or has she gone off to live with someone too?'

'I called her. I expect she'll be down when she's ready.'

'If she wants a lift, she'd better hurry up. I don't want to be late today.'

'I'll call her again when you've got your breakfast. You can pour some tea for me as well.' He glared at her but he poured it out. She felt satisfaction at some sort of victory. She plonked his breakfast in front of him, and went and yelled upstairs: 'Maria! Come down right now. Your breakfast's getting cold.'

Their daughter clattered down the stairs into the kitchen with her school tie hanging loosely round her neck.

'Put your tie on properly,' George instructed.

'I came to eat my breakfast while it's still hot. Can't please anyone, can I?'

'That's no way to speak to either of us,' snapped her father. She said nothing, sat down and began to eat. Nicola sat down with her breakfast and silence resumed.

'I'll have more tea,' George said.

'Help yourself,' his wife replied. Another black look, but he reached for the pot and poured it for himself. She didn't ask for another cup herself, deciding it wouldn't be wise.

'Are you ready?' he asked Maria. 'Only I need to leave soon. If you want a lift, you need to hurry.'

'I'll go by bus, thanks. I'm not ready yet.'

He nodded and left the table. He left for the dairy almost immediately. Nicola sighed. Another long, dreary day lay ahead.

9

When she awoke the next morning, Georgia wondered where she was. The reality came back to her with a thump. She sat up in the narrow, slightly lumpy bed and wondered what on earth she had done. She and Giles had spent a quiet evening together, both working silently but both enjoying each other's company. Maggie had left them alone for most of the time, as she went to work in her studio. Now she was faced with a trek to the bathroom and hoping that nobody else was in there. She knew that she was missing her own private en-suite and all her comfortable wardrobe space. She grabbed a woolly cardigan and went along to the bathroom. Someone was in there.

'Sorry,' came back Giles' voice. 'Won't be long.'

'Sorry. No hurry,' she replied, thinking

that she didn't mean it one bit. She was feeling slightly desperate, she realised. She went back to her room and waited for the sound of him coming out. At last he did and called out as he passed her. She almost ran along. Once she was showered and dressed, she went into the cosy kitchen. Nobody else was there. She put the kettle on and wondered about breakfast. Maybe she could find some cereal or bread to make toast? When the kettle boiled, she made a pot of tea, and hoped someone would come and help her to drink it. She thought about her home, and wondered if her father had left for the dairy and if he had taken Maria to school. She almost phoned home, but stopped herself. She felt she couldn't use the phone without asking, unless it was for something important. At last, Giles came in.

'Oh, you're up and dressed already.'

'Sorry. I gather you don't get up and dress right away?'

'No. I usually change out of my pyjamas when it's time to go to college.

Well, actually, I don't have pyjamas as such. I usually just wear underpants. I put this on for your sake. Need to protect your innocent eyes.' He was wearing a rather elderly tee-shirt that might have fitted him once, but was extremely tight now. He had on some cotton trousers that were baggy and possibly very comfortable.

'I appreciate your consideration,' she laughed. 'Is there any cereal, or whatever else you have for breakfast?'

'Sorry, it was finished. I think there may some bread to make toast. I said it was disorganised in this place, didn't I? Leave a note for Mum: she'll probably buy whatever you like later.'

'Maybe I should get it? It isn't really fair for her to buy stuff just for me.'

'Whatever you like. She's pretty good about it, though. I know she doesn't give the impression of being a house-wifely type, but she does know I need feeding; and, of course, she's not used to having a house-guest.'

'I'm sorry. I'll go to the bank on our

way to college and get some cash, then we'll go shopping. Or I'll go on my own if you're too busy.'

'I suppose your mother does all your shopping, does she?'

'My father brings stuff home from the dairy. There's quite a comprehensive shop there. She usually phones him during the day and says what she needs.'

'That sounds very convenient.'

'She does go shopping sometimes. Leaves the cleaner working away and goes off on her own.'

'You have a cleaner too?'

'Yes, Mrs Henders. I did say. She comes in every morning for a couple of hours. She's great. Always clears up my bathroom and never complains about the wet towels.' She realised what she was saying and shut up rather quickly. She didn't mean to sound as if she was boasting, but knew it must sound rather like that.

'You'll find life a bit different here. I usually clean round at the weekends.

Mum does it if she remembers, but when she's working, she often forgets. I take the washing to the launderette too.'

'You don't have a washing-machine, then?'

'Don't see the need. There's a modern launderette down the road. I usually take some work in with me, and can get a surprising amount done waiting for the stuff to go round and round in the machine.'

She smiled and asked him if he wanted more tea. It was all going to take a bit of getting used to. She wondered if they were actually short of money, but didn't like to ask. She needed to help out with some shopping at least.

'Georgia?' he said suddenly. 'I realise this is going to mean a lot of change for you. It isn't how you're used to living, and if you want to go back home, I really won't mind. Well, I will, but I'll understand.'

'Well, thank you, but I'm quite happy to be here with you. Anyway, it's nice not to be hassled by my parents with everything I do.'

'Feel free to phone them if you want to. Mum won't mind. As long as you don't chatter on forever.' He laughed and reached for her hand. He kissed her fingertips and she blushed. It seemed such a very sexy thing to do.

'Thank you, Giles. You're very sweet. Now, about that toast you thought you might make?'

'I don't actually think we have any bread. There may be some buns we could toast. Would they do?'

'They'd do fine. Where do you make toast? I can't see a toaster anywhere.'

'We don't have one. We use the grill on the cooker.'

'Right. I'll put it on, shall I? You find the buns and we'll toast them.'

He went foraging in the cupboard and eventually came out with a packet of somewhat stale buns.

'They'll be okay once they're toasted. Better leave one for Mum.'

'Where is she, by the way?'

'Probably fast asleep. She was working through the night, and went to bed at some ungodly hour.'

'I see. You'll hate my regular hours, then; I get up and go to bed at regular times. Largely because my family do, I suppose. Maybe it's time to forget about all that. Start keeping erratic times and live like normal people do.'

'I doubt we'd be classed as normal. Eccentric, maybe . . . well, definitely. My mother could never be called normal, not in comparison to a family like yours. As I said, if you want to go back home, I shall understand.'

'I can't. I'm afraid I've burned my boats. There's no going back from this one.'

'I'm sure they'll forgive you.'

'You don't know my father. He's a law unto himself, and certainly not the forgiving type. I think these buns are just about done. Do you have some butter for them?'

'I think so. I'll look in the fridge.'

They sat down at the table and

buttered the buns. They tasted a bit odd, but Georgia said nothing. Then it was time for them to go to college; and, without even saying goodbye to Maggie, they set off. She thought it a bit odd that Giles didn't say goodbye or leave a note, but it was up to him. She simply wasn't used to this way of living at all. She pondered it as they walked to college, and thought it had been what she had wanted. In many ways she loved the freedom of Giles and his mother, but she also enjoyed having everything done for her. She thought guiltily about leaving her wet towels in the bathroom that morning, and knew they'd still be there the next day if she didn't hang them up somewhere. It was time she learned to be self-reliant and do things for herself.

It seemed a long day. They were both working in the library.

'I'm about ready to go home,' Giles commented. 'How are you doing?'

'I can go whenever you like. I can finish this bit at home. It doesn't have to be given in for a day or two.'

'Come on, then. Let's go.'

'I need to go to the bank on our way. I think there's a branch just off our route. I've been there before.'

'Have you got your chequebook with you?'

'Yes, and the manager knows me and my father. It should be fine.'

They set off along the road; but when they reached the bank, it was past closing time.

'Damnation. Now we can't go shopping. I haven't got much cash left.'

'What exactly did you want to buy?'

'Just basic stuff. I can't keep eating all your food.'

'Don't be silly. Tell me what you want and I'll buy it. You can always pay me back later if you really feel the need. I'm sorry we live such chaotic lives. We're not used to having a house-guest, and it's all a bit hand-to-mouth, if you know what I mean.'

'I'm not trying to change anything. I just feel I'd like to contribute in some small way. I'll call at the station and see if I can cash in my season ticket. I'm not going to need it, am I?'

'I'd rather you kept it for a bit longer. You may need it again.'

'I can't really see why. Unless, of course, you're regretting your invitation for me to stay.'

'No, of course not. I just feel concerned that you're having to put up with things being very different to what you're used to. It must be a huge change in your life. No meals ready when you get in, and probably no food even there to use to make a meal.' She listened to his words and knew he was right. But she was determined not to give in.

'I know it's different, but I'll get used to it. I'll even learn to cook. Well, maybe that's pushing it a bit, but there are things I can do. I can probably peel carrots?' she offered.

'Wow. That's really useful. We'll always eat carrots.'

'Help us to see in the dark.'

Laughing, they walked along the road

towards Giles' home. She stopped suddenly.

'I think there's one of my father's shops somewhere here. I know it's in this area. If we go there, they'll give me credit. I'll tell them who I am and there'll be no problem. I doubt they'd even charge me for anything. Come on, I'm sure it's somewhere near here.'

'I don't like to think of you doing that. It's almost admitting you can't manage.'

'Nonsense. Maybe you know it? It'll be called Wilkins' Dairy Produce, or something like that.'

'I do know it. It's slightly more expensive than where I usually shop.'

'Where is it, then?'

'We'd have to divert from the route a bit. It's about half a mile from here.'

'Come on, then. I can't think of the name of the manager, but I'll remember when I see him, I'm sure. Brilliant, don't you think?'

'I'm not sure. I get the feeling you're expecting them to give things to you.

You don't anticipate paying, do you?'

'Come on, Giles. Don't be so utterly boring. It's my family business. Make the most of it.' She started walking in the direction he had indicated, but he lagged behind. 'Come on. I'm going anyway.'

He sighed and followed her. 'Not that street. It's the next one,' he said feebly.

Georgia was a strange girl. He was very fond of her in a way, but did find her a bit much to cope with. He was beginning to feel out of his depth with her. After all, it had been a casual invitation to move in with them, and she had jumped on it, turning up only two days later. He'd expected her to come possibly later in the term, giving them plenty of time to clear a room for her and maybe get accustomed to the idea gradually. He followed her, wondering how on earth he was going to cope when they reached the shop.

'Looks quite smart, doesn't it?' she said when they reached it. 'It's only been open a month or so. Come on in.'

'Hang on a minute. If they've only just opened, they won't know you, and you'll never get away with making demands of them.'

'Rubbish. Come on.' She went into the shop and he followed her, feeling desperately uncomfortable. 'Good evening,' she began politely. 'How are things going?'

'Quite well, thank you, ma'am.' The manager (Giles assumed) looked slightly nonplussed.

'I am Georgia Wilkins. Daughter of your boss, George Wilkins?'

'Oh, yes?' he said, not quite as politely as she would have expected.

'My father asked me to call in and see how things were going. I'm at University at present and I was passing, so here I am.'

'Well, you can tell your . . . father that everything is fine, thank you.'

'Excellent. I wanted one or two items, if that's all right.'

'Course it is, dear. Prices are all marked. Bring them over to the till and I'll check them through for you.'

'Oh yes, of course. It's self-service here, isn't it? How's that working?'

'Very well, thanks, miss. Now, what do you need?'

'Bread. Cheese. Butter. And one or two other things . . . oh yes, cereal. You won't need to put them through the till; my father wouldn't expect it.'

'I'm sorry, miss; anything that goes out of here has to be accounted for.'

'Yes, well, make a list of what I've taken and I'm sure that will be all right.'

'Oh, no you don't. How do I know what you say is true? I wasn't told anyone would be calling, and I certainly don't know you.'

'It's all right,' Giles interrupted. 'I'll pay for the goods. Come on, Georgia, leave it.'

'But . . . '

'I said, leave it.' He sounded very firm and Georgia stepped back, looking suddenly less confident. 'How much do we owe?' The manager told him and he paid up. 'Come on. Let's get home.'

Georgia felt like a naughty schoolgirl as they left the shop.

'You didn't need to do that,' she muttered.

'Well, you were clearly embarrassing the poor chap.'

'Nonsense,' she said. 'He was being objectionable. I shall tell my father how uncooperative he was.'

'Don't you dare. I thought he behaved perfectly reasonably, under the circumstances. Come on. Let's get home.' He set off at what she considered a challenging pace. He said nothing as they went along, and when they reached his home, he went straight through to see his mother in her studio. Awkwardly, she followed him.

'Hi, Maggie.'

'Hello, dear. Good day?'

'Not bad, thanks. You?'

'I'm rather behind with my work. I went shopping this morning, and it's set me back rather. I hope I've got everything you're likely to need. Get your supper when you want it. Leave mine on the side, I'll eat later.'

'Right,' said Georgia. She took the hint and went along to the kitchen, where she put the kettle on. She wondered whether to offer the others tea, but decided against it. She was seeing another side to Giles. He was quite sort of fierce in a way, and she felt rather upset by the turn of events. She looked in the fridge, and saw duplicates of everything she had collected from the shop. She felt rather guilty.

She sat and drank her tea, and decided she would do some work. Giles seemed to want to stay in his mother's studio, so she took out her books and got on with her research. She worked on till almost seven o'clock, and then wondered about their meal. She looked in the fridge again and found some chops. Maybe they were intended for their supper? She wondered what to do with them, and remembered she had seen her mother grilling them. She found the grill pan and washed it out. There was still the residue from their breakfast buns. She turned the grill on and put the chops underneath the flame. Then she thought about the rest of the meal. Potatoes. She looked around and found some, which she peeled and put into water and put onto the cooker to boil. She was pleased with her efforts so far. Vegetables. She looked for them and found carrots. She had told Giles she could peel carrots, so she set to work. Suddenly, she smelled burning and looked under the grill. The chops were singed within an inch of their lives.

'Damnation,' she grumbled, and dragged them out. She burned her fingers on the pan and dropped it on the floor. 'Oh no,' she wailed and sat down on the chair, sobbing. Giles came into the room.

'What on earth are you doing?' he demanded.

'Trying to cook supper. But I burned the chops and then they burned me.'

'You really are hopeless, aren't you?' The wretch was actually laughing at her.

'It isn't funny,' she protested. 'I've

ruined our supper; and, well, there isn't anything else. And I've got burnt fingers, too.'

'You'd better chuck the remains of the chops into the bin.' He looked in the fridge and saw the duplicated items. 'Maybe I'll turn the meal into a cheese and potato pie. The potatoes, are they all right?'

'I think so.' She lifted the lid to see a mass of white pulp. 'Oh, dear. I think maybe you won't need to mash them. They've already mashed themselves.'

He sighed.

'I think you'll be banned from the kitchen in future.'

'I *have* peeled some carrots. They're here.' She passed him several peeled carrots into his hands.

'Are we cooking them whole or chopping them up?' he asked.

'Shall I chop them into bits?'

'Maybe, if you can do that without cutting your fingers.'

She picked them up and began to chop them. They were all rather erratically-sized, and she put them into another saucepan which she gave to Giles.

'Put it onto the cooker, and don't turn it on high.'

'Sorry,' she muttered. 'I told you I was useless in the kitchen.'

'It seems you were right. We should get something to eat at *some* point.'

'Shall I lay the table?'

'You can do, but we usually eat off our knees.'

'Seems I have a lot to learn.'

'Seems you do. I suppose you always ate at the table?'

'Oh, yes. Mummy would never allow us to eat off our knees. Not even to watch television. We always ate rather formally; with vegetable dishes, too. Such a waste of time, I always thought.'

He was grating a heap of cheese while chatting, and he picked up the pan of potatoes and tried to tip out some of the water. He gave up and tipped the cheese into the pan and began to mix it. He then piled it into a pie dish and put it into the oven. In the meantime, she had thrown away the chops and was busily cleaning up the mess.

'I promise never to try to cook again, not without you to supervise me.'

'That's good. An excellent idea.'

'That cheese pie smells gorgeous. I'm starving.'

10

George sat in his office talking to Henry. They had finally agreed to allow Mr Jones to stay and farm his land for their benefit.

'I'll give him a call and get him to come in and see us. If he agrees to our terms, he can stay there.'

'Right. I guess we'll need to convince Michael and Dad, but I don't see it as being too much of a problem. Michael was reasonably in favour. What changed your mind?'

'We didn't have any replies to our advert. Thinking it over, I can't see any real reason not to employ him.'

'I agree. Right, well, I'll leave you to it. There's trouble brewing, by the way. The men in the bottling plant are getting restless.'

'How do you mean?'

'Not sure, but they've called a

meeting for lunchtime.'

'What sort of meeting?'

'There's a union rep coming in. That's all I know.'

'But there is no union here. We've always dealt with them direct. In any case, which union are they talking about?'

'I'll let you know. Possibly Transport and General Workers', or something like that.'

'Make sure you do. I won't have the men getting belligerent about anything. If they have a problem of any sort, surely they can come to me? Us. Damnation, I won't have it.' George felt furious that his workers could even consider joining any sort of union. It always spelt trouble. 'I'll go down and talk to some of them. Does your James know anything about all this?'

'I doubt it. He's been out delivering lately. I'll ask him when he's back.'

'About time he was moved on somewhere else, isn't it?'

'We need to recruit another chap for the rounds. When we find someone suitable, he can move on to somewhere else.'

Henry left him to his thoughts. He called for his secretary and asked her to write to Mr Jones, inviting him to come in again.

'Don't say why, just ask him to come in. One or two problems to sort out first. Leave the letter on my desk, I'll sign it later. Meantime, I'm going down to the bottling plant. See if I can sort out what's wrong down there.'

Everything seemed to be working normally as he arrived at the start of the line. Always fascinated by the march of milk bottles along the conveyor belts, he stood watching their progress. He wandered on until he came to the filling area. The bottles stood in small rubber cups to prevent them from tipping over, and were pressed up to the taps on the large tank above. They were then capped and passed along to the crates. He spoke to one of the operatives, or rather shouted at him.

'Everything going smoothly?'

'Sorry, sir? Can't hear you!' The rattle of all the bottles being dumped into their crates was pretty deafening.

'All okay?' he shouted again. The man nodded. He gave up trying to have any sort of conversation, and went along to the end of the line where it was a little quieter. The man working there avoided looking at him directly, making himself suddenly very involved with seeing to the crates being loaded onto the milk floats.

'Can I have a word, Benson?' he shouted.

'I'm rather busy at the moment.'

'Yes, I know you are.' The man was looking somewhat shifty and clearly didn't want to speak to him. 'But you can break off for a minute or two.'

'All right. What did you want?'

'Is there something going on down here?'

'The usual.' This man was so surly, George felt even angrier.

'So why do you have some union rep coming in to talk to you? What's wrong with the system we've always had? You can always talk to me about anything wrong.'

'We're just standin' up for our rights.'

'And what exactly do you mean by that?'

'We 'as rights. Jus' wanna talk about it. That's it.'

'I think you'd best come up to my office. We can talk there.'

'I'd rather not. I want to hear what this chap says. There's a lot of us goin' to 'is meetin'. It's not all lovely 'ere, you knows.'

'Then I want to hear about it. I need to know what's upsetting you. There's no need to call in some person who knows nothing at all about the industry.'

''E knows about our rights.'

'I want to know about what you think are your rights. How are we failing to fulfil them?'

'I'll let you know this a'ternoon. After we've seen the rep. Now, if you'll let me gerron . . . '

George sighed and left him to

'gerron'. He wandered outside to the loading bay and saw the crates being put on the backs of the floats. They had the most modern electric floats, capable of delivering to their areas. Some of them had cold-boxes too, to take butter and eggs out with them. They'd all have left in the next hour or so, and be delivering to another lot of homes in the area. He felt proud seeing them all lined up, ready to go. He knew exactly what his father had done in setting up this dairy, from its very early days when they'd had only two floats to go out and relied on people coming to the store to collect their milk.

Back inside once more, he went up to his office and saw the letter he'd requested lying on his desk. He signed it and took back to his secretary.

'Have you heard anything about this union rep who is coming in?' he asked.

'I was told, but I'm not going down. It seems as though they're not happy with things down in the bottling plant. I shouldn't really say anything.'

'No, please do continue. I need to know of any problems.'

'I think it may be a case of greed. They want an increase in payment for what they do. Some want more than others for taking on responsibilities they consider unfair. But I didn't tell you any of this. I only heard about it because, well, I happened to overhear some of them talking.'

'Thank you. I'll shall certainly be discreet. I feel saddened that they didn't come straight to me. Or one of my brothers. We'll always listen to their requests.'

He sat thinking for a while, before calling Henry and Michael to his office. He outlined what he knew of the situation and asked for their opinions.

'All a fuss over nothing,' was Henry's view.

'We could offer them all a blanket rise. A little bit extra on their hourly rate. Be worth it to avoid a strike.'

'I agree with you. I suppose we'll have to call a board meeting for their approval. At least put it past Geoffrey.'

'How much will it cost on the whole? A thousand or two at most. Surely we can afford that?'

'I'll phone Geoffrey and ask his advice. That way we'll be covered. If he wants a board meeting, I'll say it's urgent, and ask him to come in today perhaps?'

'I do feel it's up to us to make the decision without the Aunts being involved.'

'So do I, but they won't see it that way. They'll see it as money they could have had being wasted.'

'Shows how little they know about the company, doesn't it?'

'Did you ever think anything different? No, they are very keen on getting their money and not taking any real responsibility. Right, well, having agreed that between ourselves, I'll ring Father and see what he says. With any luck, I can make them an offer later today.'

He dialled his father's number and waited to hear his stentorian voice.

'Yes?' it came back to him.

'Father, George speaking. I need to have your approval on a matter.'

'Right. Go ahead,' he shouted. He seemed to think shouting was necessary for him to be heard.

'We have a problem in the bottling plant. I gather they want a pay rise. The three of us have decided to give them a small increase in their hourly rate and wanted your approval.'

'You have decided. I'm sorry, not agreeable to me. Need to organise a board meeting.'

'It is rather urgent. Can you come in this afternoon?'

'No, I have arrangements. Tomorrow, or maybe the next day.'

'We need to decide it very quickly. They have some union rep coming in at lunchtime. I want to avoid any of them signing up with him. Once we have unions involved, it makes any sort of negotiating difficult.'

'I can see that. I can't really put off my arrangements. Have you tackled your Aunts?'

'No. I came to you as the senior member.'

'Very well, I'll come in tomorrow morning. You'd better call the Aunts and see if they want to be involved.'

'If you really think it's necessary. Very well, I'll see you at nine o'clock tomorrow morning. Goodbye.'

'Yes.' He put the phone down.

'Damn,' muttered George. Typical of his father. He supposed he could understand his wish to be involved in every small detail, but to be told to invite the Aunts as well — really, it was too bad. He phoned them and spoke to May.

'We need an extraordinary board meeting tomorrow morning. Please be here at nine o'clock sharp.'

'Nine o'clock? Oh no, dear, that is much too early for us. Make it the afternoon as usual.'

'I'm sorry, but we wanted it today. Father said tomorrow is his first chance, so we're going with that.'

'We're seeing him this afternoon for tea. We can discuss it then.'

'He's taking tea with you two?' George almost shouted. 'Really, that is ridiculous. You could all come in here this afternoon.'

'Oh no, dear, Janet has made some cakes especially.'

'Bring the damned cakes in with you then. I'll send a car for you at three o'clock. Goodbye.' He slammed the phone down and re-dialled his father.

'The Aunts are coming this afternoon. Do you need me to send a car for you, or will you drive yourself? I gather you were only going for tea with them. This is a lot more important than afternoon tea.' His father made no reply. 'So, do you need a car?'

'I'll drive myself. What time?'

'Three o'clock. Thank you.' Again, he slammed the phone down, irritated beyond measure. He called his two brothers and passed on the message to them. His phone rang again.

'Yes?' he snapped, expecting someone to complain.

'It's the Highgate shop on the phone,

sir. They want to speak to you.'

'Very well. Put them through. Yes? How can I help?'

'Good morning, sir. I'm sorry to bother you, but I thought you should know. A young person claiming to be your daughter came into the shop yesterday. She wanted a lot of items on credit; well, not exactly on credit. As you know, sir, we don't do credit. She wanted me to give them to her. I said I had no idea who she really was, and so I refused her. The young man with her paid for the things, but I got the feeling he wasn't too pleased with her.'

'Really, I can't be bothered by all this. You were quite right to refuse her. I've no idea if it was my daughter or not. Is that it?'

'Yes, sir. Sorry to have disturbed you, sir. Thank you, sir.'

George put the phone down. 'Yes sir, yes sir, three bags full, sir.' He laughed. Typical Georgia! Just the sort of thing she would do. He wondered how she really was. It seemed an age since he'd seen her, but it really wasn't long. He hoped she was getting enough to eat, in view of her trying to get supplies from the store. Really, it was of no concern to him. He went back to his problems with his workers. He desperately wanted to know what was going on in the canteen, but knew he would be spotted if he actually went there, as would either of his brothers.

Lunchtime came and went. He walked down to the bottling plant once more, but everyone was working. Nobody acknowledged him, and he left again and went along to the boardroom. His secretary had arranged for tea and coffee, according to his instructions, and he stood waiting for the arrival of his Aunts and father. He did wonder if he might have panicked somewhat in getting them to come so soon, but he had decided to ask them and here he was.

Michael and Henry came into the room and his father followed them. At last the Aunts arrived, flustered by the change to their plans.

'I really don't know what all the hurry is about,' complained Janet.

'Indeed, no,' echoed May. 'What's the problem?'

'Get yourselves some tea and let us make a start,' instructed George. It took a few more minutes of fussing and drama before they had all sat down.

'This emergency meeting was called to counteract the men possibly joining a union. We have never had one in the company before, and I want to avoid it now. A union rep came into the canteen over the lunch break, and I don't want him persuading our people that this is the only way to go. I therefore want to increase the wages of our workers, and thought it would need to be passed by the board.'

'Oh, dear me, no,' said May. Janet agreed with her.

'Good. That's something positive,' began George.

'No, I mean we can't possibly approve of the men getting more money. Oh, dear me, no.'

'No, that's right,' echoed Janet.

'Oh, for heaven's sake,' Henry said out loud. 'Whyever not?'

'We can't afford to just hand out money like that. I mean, what are they going to do to make it up to us? I know we can't manage on any less.'

'You're not being asked to.'

'Father. What are your thoughts?'

'I'd say, if it means avoiding a strike, then go ahead. Give them an extra few pence an hour. We really don't want unions here. We've always prided ourselves on having good relationships with everyone.'

'Oh, dear me,' said May hurriedly. 'We didn't know you were intending to vote in favour, Geoffrey dear.' They muttered to each other, and then May spoke again. 'Very well. As long as we board members aren't going to lose out, we don't see there is a problem.'

'Excellent. I shall work out exactly what we're going to offer, and call the foremen into my office. Any other business? No? Then I declare the meeting closed.'

'Is that it?' asked May.

'Indeed, yes. All done. We needed your votes to agree to a pay rise. Now we can go ahead with it all. Thank you for coming.'

'But what about my cakes?' wailed Janet. 'I packed them up carefully and brought them with me.'

'Feel free to stay here and enjoy them, Aunt Janet. We have to get on with the working day. To my office, now, gentlemen.'

The three brothers left the boardroom and went along to George's office. They quickly agreed to the price they were going to offer, and Michael went to the bottling plant to collect the main organisers of the union rep's visit.

An hour later and it was all settled. The men's pay rise was accepted, and the union threats were all over. The three brothers congratulated themselves, and George opened a bottle of wine to celebrate properly.

'Jolly good show, I'd say. Here's to

us. The final bill should be quite manageable, and it's certainly a comfort to know there will be no union here.' They raised their glasses and drank to the company.

Feeling rather benign, George set off for home slightly earlier than usual. He must remember to tell Nicola about the odd phone call he'd received from his Highgate store. He didn't want to think of his daughter being hungry; though in truth, as he'd thought earlier, she had made the decision herself.

He arrived home to find a blazing row in progress between his wife and Maria.

'It's Friday, for heaven's sake; I'm entitled to one evening off. I want to sit quietly watching television. What's wrong with that?'

'It's rubbish you're watching. American so-called comedy shows are not good for you.'

'But I enjoy them. *I Love Lucy* — well you have to admit it's very funny. And *The Cisco Kid* is hilarious.

'Hey, Pancho, whatcha doin' ' — '

'Really, dear, I'd have thought you were above that sort of thing.'

'Well, I'm not. And *damn* school-work: I refuse to do any more tonight.'

'What's going on?' asked George.

'Maria is being quite unreasonable,' snapped Nicola.

'No, I'm not. It's you. Just because I'm the youngest, it doesn't mean you can boss me around all the time.'

'Maria, apologise to your mother. You can't speak to her like that.'

The girl looked sulky, and sullenly murmured, 'Sorry.'

'But I am going to see something on television this evening. If not, then I'll sit in my room and maybe listen to the radio. I hope that won't offend you?'

'You should be doing some schoolwork, shouldn't you?' asked George reasonably.

'Oh lord, not you as well. I'm going to my room. And no, I don't intend to open a single book. Not this evening.' She ran upstairs and slammed her bedroom door.

'Honestly. She's getting as difficult as her sister.'

'Oh yes, Georgia went into the Highgate shop yesterday, and tried to take out a lot of food products. The manager wouldn't let her take them, and her so-called boyfriend paid up. The manager behaved rather well, I feel. He said he didn't know her at all, and thought she might be just someone trying to take stuff.'

'Oh, dear. Poor girl. Do you think she's all right? I'd hate to think of her going hungry.'

'Well, yes, I agree. But I can't imagine it really, can you? Though perhaps I was a little hasty in cancelling her bank account.'

'I didn't realise you had. Oh, dear me. She must be getting desperate.'

'I'm not sure whether she's cleared the account or not. Perhaps I should pay something in for her.'

'Oh yes, please do, dear. How was your day?'

'Excellent. The Board meeting went

well, and they approved our suggestion of a pay rise for all the workers. The Aunts were against it, but when Father agreed, so did they. Honestly, two better yes-women couldn't be found.'

'Pity they're still there. Couldn't you get rid of them?'

'No chance. They'll stick it out till one of them drops off the planet.'

'Oh, dear. I don't like to think of them like that.'

'Oh, they enjoy their power, as they see it. Feel involved with the running of the dairy. They do have shares in the place, after all.'

'That's a pity as well. Minority shareholders, though, aren't they?'

'Very much so. Still gives them equal voting rights, however. Now, let's have a drink. We're done with the men joining any union, too. Great relief, I must say. I'm going to have a large Scotch and soda. What do you want, dear?'

'I'll have a glass of sherry, then I must get on with dinner. It won't take me long to put it together.'

'Excellent. Let's go and watch the news. See what's been going on in the wide world.'

They went into the dining room and Nicola sat down, having put on the television. George handed her a drink and they both settled down to watch. Moments later, Maria joined them.

'Don't I get offered a drink? Seems you're both celebrating something.'

'There's plenty of orange juice in the fridge. Help yourself.'

'I was thinking of a sherry.'

'Nonsense. You're too young.'

'I'm nearly eighteen. I bet you'd had plenty to drink by my age.'

'All right,' agreed George. 'You can have a small sherry.' He got up and poured it for her. Smugly, she sat down and sipped it. One small victory won, she felt happier.

11

Saturday in Highgate, almost a week after Georgia had left her home, proved slightly boring for the girl. She wasn't sure what she had been expecting, but Giles had decided to do some painting. As she didn't have anything much to do, she wandered round the house at a loose end.

'I might go shopping,' she said to the pair who were working in the studio.

'Okay. See you later,' said Giles.

'Can you pick up something for supper this evening?' asked Maggie.

'Sure. Anything in particular?'

'You choose something you'd like.'

'Right,' she said uncertainly, wondering how she was going to pay for it. She was planning to have a wander round the clothes shops, and if she found something, she would pay for it by cheque. The banks were all closed on a

Saturday, so she couldn't actually draw any cash out. She didn't like to ask anyone for cash, and she certainly wasn't accustomed to living without. For a moment, she wondered whether to go back to her home. She could always say she'd gone back to collect more clothes. Her parents wouldn't let her be short of money, surely? She still had her season ticket which meant she could travel for nothing. She had meant to cash it in, but somehow she hadn't found the time or inclination. Had she made a disastrous mistake in moving out? Though she was enjoying the freedom, she was certainly missing some things.

'Actually, I think I may go back home and collect some more clothes.'

'As you like, dear,' Maggie said absently.

Georgia wasn't sure they had both heard her. Giles was rather involved in his painting and he nodded to her.

'Have fun,' he murmured.

'Thanks,' she replied, wondering how

on earth he thought it might be fun. 'Okay then. I'll get off.'

'Bye,' the two painters said together.

Feeling slightly despondent, she walked along the road towards the station. It took her quite a while to get to the main line where she could catch her train home. During the ride, she wondered how her parents would take her coming back. At least her father would be at work, though he usually came home at midday. Could she collect enough things by the time he returned? She doubted it. By the time she had chatted to Maria and her mother, there was no way she could miss her father.

Though she had only been away for a few days, she noticed things en route for home. Things she had always taken for granted. It really wasn't a bad place to live, she decided by the time she was walking into the drive. She gulped and swallowed hard. This was going to be difficult.

She opened the door with her own key.

'Hallo,' she called out.

'Georgia? Is that you?' called her mother from the kitchen.

'Yes.'

'Oh, darling. Welcome back. We have missed you.' She came running into the hall and embraced her like the long-lost daughter she really was.

'I've just come back to collect a few more things,' she said, feeling somewhat choked by her mother's reception.

'Oh, dear. I thought you may have decided to come back to us.'

'I'm sorry,' was all she could say.

'Okay. I understand. How's Giles?'

'He's fine. He's painting today, so I decided it would be a good thing if I came to collect my stuff.'

'I see. Would you like a coffee? I was just going to make some.'

'Thanks. Maria in?'

'She's in her room. Working, of course.'

'She's a good girl. She deserves to get to Oxford or Cambridge. I assume she still has plans to go there?'

'All being well. I'll go and put the kettle on, shall I?'

'I'll go up and see my sister. Maybe she'd like some coffee too?'

'Okay. Ask her and bring her down with you.'

Georgia ran up the wide staircase, shouting out her sister's name.

'Georgia! How lovely to see you. Are you back?'

'Only to collect some more stuff.'

'So how's it going? Do you have a room to yourself . . . or are you sharing with your boyfriend?'

'Course I have a room. It's not huge, but at least it's my own. Well, mine to use.'

'You don't sound all that happy. And where is the lovely Giles?'

'He's doing some painting.'

'Walls or canvases?'

'Canvases, of course. He's actually rather good.'

'I'd have thought you'd be doing something together. It is a Saturday, after all.'

201

'Well, he's painting. It's the only day of the week he can paint, actually. Do you want coffee?'

'I suppose so. Shall I come down?'

'I think you'd better. Mummy expects you to.'

'One must always do what Mummy expects.'

'You sound somewhat bitter.'

'Oh, don't mind me. I just get fed up with them always expecting me to work. I need a break sometimes.' She went on to tell her sister about the previous evening and the traumas she went through just to spend some time watching television.

'They love to control, don't they?' Georgia said with some bitterness. 'Why do you think I left?'

'You haven't got room for one more, have you?'

'Don't be silly. You only have another year, then it'll be off to Uni. Come on. Coffee time.'

They both went down the stairs and into the kitchen.

'I thought you'd got lost. Coffee's

ready. I thought we'd go into the lounge for it.'

'The kitchen's fine. So, tell me what's been going on. Did you go out for dinner the other day?'

'No. It was the day you left, if you remember. Your father refused to go out once you were no longer with us.'

'We had egg and chips,' Maria said bitterly.

'I did actually make omelettes,' Nicola protested.

'More or less the same. Still egg and chips.'

'I'm sorry I missed out,' smiled Georgia.

'So, tell me about your life in Highgate,' her mother asked.

'Different. It's very laid-back. They are very easy about everything; meals and cleaning and stuff don't matter to them. It's quite refreshing, actually.'

'It sounds horrendous to me.'

'Well, it would. Maggie asked me to get something for supper, and when I asked what, she just said something you fancy. Only snag is, it has to cost next to nothing.'

'Are you short of money, dear?'

'Sorry. I shouldn't have said that. It just sort of slipped out. I haven't got any cash till I've been to the bank. They're not open on Saturdays, though.'

'Your father has stopped making payments into your account. He wanted to punish you for leaving home, I think.'

'Oh, that's charming. If I was still at home, he'd pay me whatever he always did, plus my food!'

'I don't think he liked the thought of paying for everyone else's food. I'll have a word with him.'

'Well, thanks. But he is being ridiculous. I still have all my usual expenses from college; and, well, I do need to pay my way with Maggie and Giles. They're giving me a room without any extra cost to anyone.'

'I think your father feels you have a room here. Oh, I don't know, I'll see if I can spare you something. I don't actually have much cash: your father pays all our bills directly. I could perhaps give you a cheque, but that won't help you much with today's problem.'

'Thanks, Mummy. I'm sorry, I didn't mean to worry you.'

'I'll see if your father has any cash with him. He'll be home in an hour or so.'

The three sat chatting about things in general, until Georgia thought she needed to be going. She went up to her room and stuck a few extra things into a bag. She felt hesitant about staying for too long, but she knew her mother wanted her to stay and try to make up with her father. Maria has sat on her bed watching her pack.

'You've left loads of your make-up. Aren't you going to take it with you?'

'I'm thinking of giving up make-up. Maybe I'd better if I don't have any money.'

'He can't mean you to starve. I've only got about five bob left, but you can have that.'

'Oh Maria, bless you. I won't take it,

though. I suppose I'd better hang on till he comes back. Hopefully, Mummy will make him see sense.'

'My father? See sense? You are joking, of course.'

'This is true. *Seeing sense* and *our father* don't fit into the same sentence.' They both giggled helplessly. The tension was getting to them both. 'I do miss you, little sister.'

'I really miss you too. It was always rather comforting to have you in the next room if I felt like a chat. Still, I suppose you'd have been leaving after the summer anyway. Will you be coming on holiday with us this year?'

'I doubt I'll be invited. I'm just not sure what I'll be doing. Where are you going?'

'Not sure. There was talk of somewhere in the Mediterranean, but that may just be Father's fantasy.'

'I'm a bit worried about Mummy. She seems even more bored than ever.'

'I know. She relies on me far too much. Shame she couldn't get a job of some sort. Even working for a charity might get her out a bit.'

'Now, that's a good idea. Isn't there some charity shop where she could go and help out?'

'There's one in the High Street. Maybe we could suggest it. Give her some stuff to take in to sell, and she could get involved.'

'I'll look some stuff out right away. Have you got anything?'

'I'll look later.'

Georgia looked in her wardrobe and took out a few items she no longer liked. She put them on her bed and left them for her mother to collect later. 'That might get her started, anyway.'

They both went down together.

'I've put some things out for lunch. If you want to eat now, at least I'll know you're not starving.'

Georgia looked at the array of food on the kitchen table. Cold meats, pâté and cheese. There was a crusty loaf as well.

'Wow, this looks a real feast. Thanks,

Mummy. May I help myself?'

'Please do. I'd give you something for your supper, but I don't really have much in.'

'Don't worry about it. If you can spare me any money, though, that would be terrific. Oh, by the way, I've put a few things on my bed that I don't want again. I wondered if you wouldn't mind taking them to the charity shop?'

'Oh, I don't know.'

'You could maybe help out there, Mummy. They always need more ladies to go and help. It might relieve your boredom.'

'Oh no, your father wouldn't like it.'

'Would he know? I mean to say, he's always at work anyway. I think it would be a splendid idea.'

'It might be like one of those awful jumble sales. No, I don't think it would be possible.'

'I think you should have a look round when you take my stuff in.' Georgia was getting most enthusiastic about the possibility. 'They are mostly housewives like you who go to work there.'

'Really? I suppose I've never thought about it.'

'Well, you should start thinking. And don't say anything to Daddy. What he doesn't know, and all that . . . This is lovely food, Mummy. Thank you very much.'

'I think I can hear your father's car.' She went to look out of the window. 'Yes, it is. He's home quite early.'

'Hope he's in a good mood. He won't like me being here.'

'Don't say anything. Just eat,' advised Maria. Georgia laughed and did as her sister suggested.

Her father came into the kitchen. 'Oh good,' he said. 'Lunch is ready.' He seemed not to have noticed his daughter was there.

'Hello Daddy,' she said at last.

'Hello,' he replied, slightly puzzled. 'Oh. Georgia. You're back. Just as well. Your mother has been missing you.'

'I'm only here to collect some more stuff. And have lunch, of course.' He made a *hmph* sort of noise which indicated his displeasure.

'I'll take mine into my study,' he said grumpily.

'Before you do, dear, Georgia is in need of some cash. Do you have any?'

'Why does she need cash? Isn't her new home looking after her properly?'

'Of course she needs some money. Her expenses at college, for one thing. And why should someone else have to fund her food?'

'She should have thought about it before she went off.'

'Don't bother, Daddy, I'll get a job. I hear Woollies are on the lookout for new staff on Saturdays.'

'Woolworths? You can't be serious.'

'If I have to, I will.'

'I'll think about it.' He filled a plate and went off to his study.

'He gets meaner every day,' Maria suggested. 'Grumpy old thing.'

'I suppose one can't blame him. He does have the dairy to manage. He's been having problems with the board meetings. What with that and buying new farms, he's had a lot of expenditure.'

'I suppose the Aunts are giving him problems. Isn't it about time they gave up? I mean to say, what good do they do?'

'They allow your grandfather to maintain his control over the company. He sees it as his own baby. Oh, by the way, he wants to give you some shares for your twenty-first. Nothing too significant but a few so you feel involved.'

'Oh, really? That's good of him. I'm not sure exactly what that means, but I'm sure it's his generosity surfacing.'

'I think it will pay you some sort of dividend. I doubt it will make a huge difference, but he seems to think it will involve you in the actual workings of the dairy. Mind you, it was somewhat dependent on you being around here. He was disappointed at your absence on his last visit.'

'I won't be blackmailed into coming back,' Georgia said fiercely. She felt herself getting close to tears and swallowed hard to keep them at bay. 'I'd better be getting back. Thank you for lunch. It was lovely.' She rose from the table and went to pick up her bag. 'Bye Mummy. Bye Maria.' She gave them both a hug and went to the front door.

'Wait a minute, you must have some money. Let me look in my bag and see what I can spare.' She took out her wallet and removed some notes. 'Here, I can spare this. Aren't you going to say goodbye to your father?'

'I suppose so. Thanks very much, Mummy. I really do appreciate it.' She went to knock at her father's door. She heard him grunt, and opened it. 'I'm off now. Just wanted to say goodbye.'

'Do you have to go?' he asked.

'Well, yes, I do. I'm sorry,' she added.

'Very well.' He took out his wallet and handed over a bundle of notes. 'Can't think of you being hungry, however much I disapprove of what you're doing. And don't go asking in one of my shops for credit. There's a strict policy enforced: they don't allow credit.'

'How did you know?' she gasped.

'I know these things. We do miss you, Georgia. Feel free to come back and see us, won't you? And bring this young man of yours with you.'

'Goodness! Thank you, Daddy; that's very good of you. I will. And thank you very much for the cash. It will make a whole lot of difference to me.'

'I'll pay something into your bank account too. Can't have you going round looking for a meal.'

'It isn't that bad, just a bit disorganised. I don't like to keep asking for money, so this will make all the difference. Perhaps I can bring Giles over next Sunday?'

'Have a word with your mother. I'm sure that will be fine.'

'Thanks, Daddy. You're not such a bad old thing after all.'

'Less of the old, thank you.'

She went out into the hall and closed

his door. Her mother and sister were standing outside, waiting to hear what had gone on.

'Is it okay if Giles and I come round for Sunday lunch next week?' she asked.

'Oh darling, of course it is,' her mother said happily.

'And get yourself along to that charity shop on Monday. You'll enjoy it.'

She hugged them both and went out into the street, her heart feeling much lighter. Maybe it was all going to work out after all.

12

By the time she reached the station, Georgia felt exhausted. Hauling her case along was no fun at all, and she finally almost fell onto her train. She would get a taxi at the other end, she decided. Thanks to her parents' gifts of some cash, she could afford to. She could then go out again to get something for supper. Steak, she decided. They would have a treat. And she would buy some wine, really push the boat out. Feeling much more cheerful, she sat back and relaxed.

The taxi took only a few minutes to reach her new home, and she paid and gave the driver a generous tip. She had to knock at the door as she still hadn't got her own key.

'Oh, it's you,' said Giles as he opened the door. 'Come on in. Have you been home again? And is that a taxi?'

She glanced round as the taxi drove away. 'Oh, yes. I couldn't manage all this lot and my parents gave me some cash, so I thought I'd treat myself.'

'That's nice, though I'm not sure where you're going to put a load more things. I suppose I could fix up some sort of rail for you.'

'It's all right, I can live out of a suitcase for a while. I've got to go and buy something for supper; I didn't have the chance earlier.'

'Don't worry about it.'

'I'm not! I'll dump this in my room and go out before I take my coat off. How's the painting getting on?'

'Almost finished. Mum's engrossed in hers, so we may not see her again today.'

'Really? But I was going to buy something special for supper. She'll surely come out to eat, won't she?'

'One never can tell. Get something for her anyway. She can always warm it up later if she wants to work on.'

'What I'm planning won't really keep

warm. If she really won't eat with us, maybe I'd better think again.'

'Oh, don't worry. I'll tell her she really needs to come and eat with us.' Giles seemed resigned to his mother's strange ways.

'Okay. Thanks. I'll go and find the butcher's.' She went out again and walked to the nearby High Street stores. She bought three large steaks and then got mushrooms, tomatoes and various other things. She went into an off-licence and bought a bottle of nice wine, one her father favoured and which was rather more expensive than she'd realised. Not to worry, she told herself. She could always go to the bank again next week after her father had paid some more money into her account.

She really wanted to treat Giles and his mother for taking her in and making her feel so at home. At least, they had accepted her as a sort of guest; but in truth, she'd had to fit in with their way of life. Maggie was very nice, but she really did her own thing most of the time. She thought of her own mother and the way she had given her total life to her husband and family. She really hoped her mother would go and work in the charity shop as Maria had suggested. She walked back to Giles' and Maggie's house, feeling very weary after her busy day. She knocked at the door again, and this time Maggie opened it.

'Hi there, Georgia. Oh, good, you've been shopping; I was just about to go out myself.'

'You did ask me to buy something for supper.'

'Did I? Sorry, I must have been in one of my dreams. We'll need something for tomorrow as well so I'll have to go anyway.'

'I'm sorry. I only bought stuff for supper tonight. I never thought of tomorrow. I have bought something special for tonight, anyway. I'll probably need some help with cooking it, but then Giles is rather good, isn't he?'

'I don't know about him being good. He can cook the basics: case of needs-must or starve! I'm sorry, I don't suppose you're used to having to live like we do. I expect you've got the sort of mother who looks after you all properly.'

'I wish she'd relax a bit, actually. She has nothing in her life except her family. I've suggested she goes and tries the local charity shop, as they always need helpers. I'm afraid she's very bored.'

'Goodness me. What luxury to actually have the time to feel bored.'

Georgia stared at her. She had never thought of it like that. Maybe her mother wasn't really benefiting from her life of luxury by simply feeling bored. Maggie would love to relax and not have to be working so hard. On the other hand, perhaps Maggie *did* relax when she was painting, and it was an overwhelming thing that she felt compelled to do.

'Shall I put the kettle on for a cup of tea?' she asked.

'Why not? The shops won't close for

a while, and I may even get a bargain if I go later. They often do have things that are going to be left over.' Georgia smiled and put the kettle on.

The two women sat companionably drinking tea. They were chatting easily about various things, and then Maggie stood up.

'Better go now or they'll be closing.'

'Thanks for the chat,' Georgia said. 'It was nice to learn a bit more about you and Giles. He never really talks about things.'

'I know he's very fond of you. I hope you're not going to let him down.'

'Of course I'm not. In fact, my parents have asked us round for lunch next Sunday. That's really something, for them to feel they want to meet one of my friends. You should come too — I'll phone and ask if it's all right.'

'Oh no, dear, I shall enjoy a quiet day on my own. You take Giles and let them all meet each other without his odd mother hanging on.'

'Oh, Maggie. You're not at all odd. I

just wish my parents were a bit more like you.'

'Careful what you wish for. I'm going now, or there'll be nothing to eat tomorrow.' She went off and Georgia washed their mugs under the tap. She went into the studio and saw Giles staring at his painting.

'What's wrong?' she asked him.

'It's the perspective. It's somehow slightly off. This building in the distance is slightly too strong.'

'Maybe you can paint over it somehow. Blur it into the background more.'

'Maybe . . . I'll leave it for now, let it dry off. One thing about oils, you can easily paint over it later. Come on, let's see what you've bought for supper.'

'I got some steak. And all the trimmings. I don't quite know what to do with them all, though.'

'Wow. You must have spent a fortune. This wine, too . . . it's rather a good one, isn't it?'

'It's one my father likes. I suppose it

was a bit expensive. But he gave me some money and so did Mummy. Did you hear me telling your Mum? They've invited us both for Sunday lunch next week. That was really something, I felt.'

'Oh, dear. I'm not sure.'

'How do you mean?'

'I'm not sure I'm quite ready for that. Suppose they hate me?'

'Why on earth would they do that? Don't worry about it. You've got a whole week to get ready for it. They aren't really so bad, you know.'

'But you've got a posh house and a mother who is always at home doing things for everyone.'

'Oh please, Giles. Don't see them as the enemy.'

'My goodness, you've changed your mind. This time last week they couldn't do anything to please you. You said they were control freaks who wanted to ruin your life. What's changed?'

'They're not that bad. Did I actually say they were control freaks?'

'You did indeed.'

'Sorry, Mummy and Daddy,' she said to the roof. 'They actually gave me some money and seemed much better about me living here.'

'Well, I'm glad about that. All right, I'll come with you next week. Now, let's get ourselves organised to cook supper. You can wash the potatoes and we'll put them to bake. Can you chop onions? And you can wash the mush-rooms . . . heavens, how many did you buy?'

'A pound. Isn't that right?'

'Er . . . possibly about twice what we need! No worries, I expect they'll come in handy later in the week.' He set to work sorting things out, and Georgia scrubbed the potatoes.

'What do you want me to do with the onions?'

'Peel them and slice them. You don't know how to do that, do you?'

'Sorry, I've never peeled an onion in my life.'

'Oh, dear me. You are so sadly lacking in cooking skills, aren't you?'

She felt hurt by his comments and then saw his face as he tried to stifle a grin. She thumped him in a friendly way and he caught her hands. Holding them behind her back, he leaned forward and kissed her. She kissed him back, feeling her world turning upside down with pleasure. She wriggled her arms free and put them round his neck, drawing him even closer.

'Oh Giles,' she whispered. 'I do love you.'

'I love you too. Dearest Georgia. Now, back to peeling onions and stop distracting me from the tasks in hand.'

'You'll have to show me what to do.' He grinned and stood behind her; his hands reaching forwards and holding her hands, he showed her how to peel and chop the onions. 'My eyes are watering,' she told him.

'So are mine.' They both laughed, and that was how they were standing when Maggie came back.

'Don't mind me,' she said, coming into the kitchen and dumping her bag down on the table. 'I managed to get a nice joint of lamb. He knocked quite a bit off the cost too. What are you two doing?'

'Cooking supper,' said Georgia meekly. 'Giles is showing me what to do.'

'I'll leave you to it. I've got a few things I need to finish.' She left them and they both giggled again. Supper took them a long time to prepare.

★ ★ ★

Back at Georgia's home, her parents spent a rare afternoon in the garden. Nicola decided the only way she could communicate with her husband was to spend time with him while he was gardening. He was working in the greenhouse, potting small plants for the vegetable plot. For once, she was less critical of his activities than usual.

'What are they going to be?' she asked.

'Cauliflowers. I'm putting them into pots so Hawkins can plant them out in a week or two. Then we'll have them in the winter months.'

'Lovely. I must say, the garden is coming on nicely. The antirrhinum are growing beautifully. George, can I ask you something?'

'Course. What do you want?'

'I was thinking . . . It was something Georgia said this morning. She suggested I might go and do a stint in the charity shop. Would you have any objection?'

'Why on earth would you want to do that?' he asked.

'Something to do. It's a worthwhile cause, too. I was thinking it would get me out for a morning or two.'

'Up to you, dear.'

'Good. I'll go and take some things there and see if they could do with my help.' She smiled quietly to herself. Her daughter was right. She really did need some interest outside the house. 'Don't forget, she and Giles are coming to Sunday lunch next week, by the way. I thought we should at least show a bit of interest in the people she's living with.'

'You don't think there's anything going on, do you?'

'Knowing Georgia, no. I think she's got her head screwed on. She may think she's living the life of Riley, but I think she knows what she's doing. I'm looking forward to meeting this young man. We can then decide how we approach her in future.'

'Load of fuss over nothing. Mark my words, she'll come back with her tail between her legs before she's done.'

'I hope you're right. I suppose I'd better go and start dinner soon.'

'What are we having?'

'I got some nice steaks from the butcher. I'll do them how you like them. Jacket potatoes or chips?'

'Chips, I think. I don't really mind.'

'You know, I'm horribly afraid that Georgia won't ever come back home. Not properly.'

'Up to her.'

'Well, I know it is. But you have to admit, she does seem to have settled in that hippy environment. I really can't understand it. We've given her everything she could possibly want. She had a lovely room and a sizeable dress allowance. Her meals are always ready for her when she comes in, and her laundry is always done and ready for her.'

'Yes, well, you always have spoilt her.'

'Maybe; but you must admit, I do the same for you.'

'Well, you're married to me. It's expected a wife will look after her husband. Now, if you'll excuse me, I want to go outside and do some work on the flowerbeds.'

Nicola sighed. He was always the same. They didn't really have a proper relationship, not as normal married couples did. She didn't think his brother's wives were any different. It must be the way they had been brought up. George had seemed like such a good catch when they were married, and she knew most of their friends thought she was so very lucky. She watched him collecting a garden fork and begin to dig in one of the flower beds. No doubt he was about to plant exact lines of flowers, and woe betide them if any of them didn't bloom in their neat row. She would like to have seen them scattered randomly around the garden, but that would never do for her husband. She went back into the house and began to prepare things for dinner.

Maria came down from her room.

'What are you doing?' she asked.

'Just preparing stuff for dinner.'

'Have we got any cake? I need something to eat. And a drink. Shall I put the kettle on?'

'Why not? I'll see what I can find for us to eat ... Maria, do you think Georgia will ever come back home?'

'Course she will. You're having them over for Sunday lunch next week, aren't you?' Maria wondered why her mother was asking her such questions. 'She'll be looking for a job in the summer. She finishes Uni then anyway, and then she'll need to work at something, won't she?'

'Has she talked about this to you?'

'Not really. I think she'll be looking at working in an art gallery or a museum. Something to use her degree, anyway.'

'I think your father was hoping she'd work in the dairy somehow.'

'What? I don't think so. I can't see her shoving milk crates around for the rest of her life, can you?'

'He was thinking of some sort of office job, I believe.'

'Oh, Mummy. Be serious. I can't think of anything she could do in that place. Forget it; I think your eldest is destined for other things. Shall I made a pot of tea, or mugs?'

'Oh, let's have mugs. And there's some cake in the tin over on the side. Let's have a picnic.'

The two of them sat companionably at the kitchen table, eating and drinking.

'Better not have any more or we'll

never manage dinner later,' Nicola announced.

'Maybe not. This cake is rather good, though. I could easily manage another piece.'

'You'll get fat. It's not as if you get a lot of exercise.'

'I do at school. They're always on at us to play games or bounce around the gymnasium. I do actually quite enjoy it; I'm always knackered after it.'

'Maria. That's no way to talk.'

'Well, I am. Whatever phrase you want me to use.'

'*Exhausted* will do nicely.'

'The other girls would laugh if I said that. *Knackered* is standard at our school.'

'Oh dear, times have certainly changed. I'd better get on with dinner now. Your father will want to eat when he gets in.'

'Let him wait for a bit. Do him good.'

'Oh, I couldn't do that. He'd be cross.'

'You should let him. Make him appreciate you a bit more. You really do martyr yourself for him. For all of us, really. I'd never do that for my husband; if I ever get one, of course.'

'Why wouldn't you?'

'Well, if I do get to Oxford or Cambridge, I'll become a bluestocking. They never get married, do they? Just have affairs with other women or be dramatic and sit around talking about it.'

'I don't know where you get your ideas from. It all sounds rather ridiculous to me. I hope you'll go to one of them. You deserve it after all the hard work you do.'

'At least you'll have something to put on my tombstone. 'She worked very hard'.'

'Really, Maria. You do have some very strange ideas.'

'Well, I always thought I'd die young.'

'Now you're being silly, dear. There's no reason you should die at all. Let's change the subject right away. I won't have you talking like that.'

'Sorry Mummy. I think I'll go and

see how Daddy's getting on. I'll put the mugs in the sink, shall I?'

'Leave them on the table. I need the sink to prepare the vegetables.'

Nicola watched as her daughter went out into the garden. She was such a lovely girl and so clever. She suddenly felt jealous of her future: university and a career that held a whole bright lifetime ahead. It was terrible to feel jealous like that, but she really couldn't help it. Her own schooldays had been spent in boarding schools, which she had quite enjoyed. But so much of the time she had spent walking with books balanced on her head to give her correct deportment, and sewing lessons which were designed to help her make clothes. There had been nothing like the sort of things Maria was learning. Remembering the rows they'd had when schools were being decided, she was glad they'd allowed the girls to make their own choices. They had both decided they preferred to stay at home rather than board. It seemed to work reasonably well for both of them.

She sighed and continued to peel potatoes. At least she knew how to put on a good meal. And on Monday, she had definitely decided to go to the charity shop. Who knew where that might lead?

13

It was a happy evening in Highgate. Giles and Georgia had cooked their meal together and invited Maggie through when it was all ready.

'I say, you really did buy us a lovely meal,' said Maggie. 'I now feel guilty at asking you to get something. I should have given you some cash.'

'No worries. My parents both gave me some. I wanted to say thank you.'

'I'm not sure why. We haven't really done much to make you feel at home. I even had to go and buy some sheets for your bed before you came.'

'Really? I'm sorry, I didn't realise.'

'You can take them to the launderette tomorrow if you like. Plus anything else you need to wash of course.'

'Really?' She then remembered Giles saying he usually took their washing to the launderette. 'I can take anything else if I go.'

'We'll both go tomorrow,' Giles agreed.

'But it's Sunday. Will they be open?'

'Course.'

'You can go in the morning while I'm cooking. Be nice for Giles to have company for once.'

Georgia smiled. It would be a new experience for her, and make a change from the usual neat piles of laundry she was used to finding in her room at home. She wondered about ironing. She had no skills at that, and wondered if Maggie would do hers as well as her own.

'What happens about drying it and ironing?' she asked.

'Oh, it usually goes in the tumble-dryer,' Giles reassured her. 'We never iron anything.'

'Really?' she said feeling astounded. 'I'd never have known it.'

'Comes out the tumbler reasonably smooth. A bit of smoothing before you put it away, and there you are.'

'Okay, if you say so. What time do you want to go?'

'As soon as we're up and ready. Tell you what, I'll stand us breakfast at the little cafe while it's washing. It takes an hour or so.'

'Really? Okay. Thank you.'

'You must stop saying *Really?* as if it's something amazing I've suggested,' he teased.

'Sorry. You are unusual, though; the pair of you. Lovely but different.'

'And so are you.' He reached over the table and took her hand. She looked at Maggie, feeling slightly embarrassed.

'Don't mind me, I'm going to do the washing-up now. You two go into the lounge. You cooked it all, so it's only fair.'

'Thanks, Mum. Come on, then.'

'Are you sure?'

'Quite sure. Go on with you.' She smiled at the two of them, remembering her own courtship. They had it so much easier these days, both staying in the same house for a start. She and her own husband had lived a long way apart and, until they were actually married, had spent little time together alone. It had been a good marriage, though it had been brought to an abrupt end with the war. She gave a little sigh. At least she had been left with a beautiful boy, and she really hoped that Georgia didn't let him down. She liked the girl well enough, but she was the first real girlfriend he'd had. She hoped her privileged background wasn't going to spoil things for them. All seemed well at the moment, but she certainly did have her concerns. Perhaps she should have taken up Georgia's offer to take her with them for lunch next Sunday. But she knew it wasn't the most sensible idea, and continued with the washing-up.

In the lounge Giles was sitting close to his girl. He pulled her closer to him and kissed her. Though she responded to him, there was something holding her back.

'What is it? What's wrong?' he asked.

'Nothing. I just don't want your mum to come in and see us.'

'Oh, Georgia, don't worry. She wouldn't mind. Why do you think she sent us in here in the first place?'

'I don't know. I suppose you're right. But we mustn't get carried away. You know we shouldn't.'

'Of course I know. I haven't . . . well, I haven't ever . . . oh, you know.'

'Nor have I. Not for lack of invitations, I should add.'

'Oh yes, and who were they from?'

'Various boys I met at the dances I used to go to. My father always approved of such stuffed shirts, and if ever I'd said yes, he'd have had me at the altar right away.'

'Heavens. You must find this all a bit of a come-down,' he murmured, moving a little further away from her.

'I love you, Giles. I really mean it. I don't want anything to go too far yet, though. I like you and the way you live, and your mum is wonderful. She's so brave. It must have been so difficult for her, after . . . well, after your father was killed.'

'I suppose so. But she always had her painting to get home to. I've said before, I don't really remember him. I was only about five when he went away. I was starting school as well, and that seemed to occupy my mind much more than Dad being away.'

'Where did you go to school?'

'Oh, it was just the local primary. Doesn't exist any more. All a bit primitive in a way: peculiar toilets across the playground, you know the sort of thing.'

'Not really.'

'I suppose you went to a private school?'

'Well, yes. It was very small and, well, very nice.'

'The daughters of gentlefolk, no doubt.'

'Now you're mocking me.'

'Come here. Kiss me properly and shut up.' She did as she was told.

The next morning, Georgia packed her dirty clothes into her bag and took the sheets off the bed. She put her towels into the bag and took it into the kitchen.

'Oh, good. You're up then.'

'Obviously. I've got all my dirty stuff.'

It was a different way to spend a Sunday morning. Sitting in the launderette watching the washing go round in the machine very soon became boring.

'I promised you breakfast. Come on. This will take at least another half hour or more before we have to put it in the tumble-dryer.'

They went to the little cafe nearby and both had a bacon roll and coffee. It tasted wonderful.

'This is the first time I've ever eaten breakfast in a place like this. I've really enjoyed it, even if my mother would have died rather than be seen here. Shall we get back to the washing now?'

Once it was dried, they both folded and smoothed their things and took them home. It was all new to Georgia, and, she had to admit, she had rather enjoyed it all. Her clothes might not be ironed within an inch of their lives, but who cared? They were all wearable and clean.

She quickly fitted into the routine at Highgate. Soon it was the following Sunday, and their trip to see her parents loomed.

'You're sure about this?' asked Giles.

'Course. My parents want to meet you and make sure you don't have two heads, or anything else peculiar.'

'Okay, well, I'll tuck the other head into my shirt. Oh, do I need a tie? Only I don't really have one . . . '

'Course not. Just go as yourself. As long as you're clean and tidy, my mother will love you. Father is a different matter. He'll question you about your morals and future prospects, just to make sure you don't expect to get a load of money from marrying me. Oops, sorry, I'm pre-empting things a bit.'

'Marrying you? I hadn't even thought that far ahead. I'm afraid I couldn't afford even a curtain ring at the moment, let alone an engagement ring.'

'I'm sorry. I shouldn't have said that.

Forget it, please.'

'But you've obviously thought about it.'

'Not really. I was just saying something rather obvious; at least, as far as my family are concerned. They'll want to know all about you.'

'Now I really am worried. I'm just a poor student, don't forget.'

'A very sexy one.' He frowned. 'Come on, I'm teasing you. I know exactly who you are and I happen to like it a lot. Don't worry, I'm not expecting a proposal. Really, I'm not.' She spoke very earnestly and hoped he understood. The look on his face suggested to her that he didn't.

'I'd better go and change. I hope this is going to work out.' He went off looking rather worried, and she felt awful. Why on earth had she mentioned the dreaded word *marriage?* It really had just slipped out, and she had no real thoughts on the matter. For goodness sake, he was only her boyfriend, wasn't he? Okay, so she loved him, and he'd said he loved her, but that was it. He came back a few minutes later, wearing a smart shirt and jacket but no tie.

'You do scrub up well,' she said lightly. 'Shall we go?'

'Into the jaws of death and all that. I really hope you know what you're doing.'

'I'm taking the man I love home to meet my parents. They will love you too. Honestly.'

They walked along the road towards the station, holding hands and talking.

'I ought to have got some flowers or something for your mother.'

'Course not. They've got flowers in the garden. Just try to relax and accept you're just going out for Sunday lunch. Okay?'

'I'll try. You should hear how fast my heart's beating, though. I feel very nervous.'

They arrived at her parents' home just before midday. Everyone seemed somewhat nervous and tense. Even George seemed not to be coping particularly well.

'Come in, my boy. Would you like a sherry?'

'Well, er . . . Thank you, sir.' Giles actually disliked sherry, but it seemed churlish to refuse.

'Georgia? You want some?'

'I'd rather have wine if you've got some. I think Giles might prefer that too.' He shot her a look of gratitude.

'Right. I'll go and get some.' He went off to the kitchen and they all relaxed. Maria was eyeing Giles, and smiled at him.

'Don't look so nervous. Daddy may seem a bit ferocious, but he's quite a pussycat really.'

'Pussycat? No way can you think of him as a pussycat.'

'I was thinking more of a tiger type of cat?' They all giggled.

'I'm sure he's fine. I never really had a father. Mine died during the war.'

'Oh, wow. That's tough. You just live with your mum now don't you?'

'Yes. We get on pretty well. She's a bit eccentric, I suppose, but who isn't?'

George came back into the room carrying an opened bottle of red wine. He poured out a couple of glasses and handed them over.

'Don't I get any?' asked Maria.

'Certainly not. You can have fruit juice. Go and get some from the fridge.'

'How thrilling,' she said as she went out.

'So, what do you intend to do next?' George asked their visitor.

'I hope to get a job, of course, once I've finished at Uni. Some sort of curator's type job at a big art gallery.'

'Really? That sounds a bit dull.'

'Not at all, Daddy. It's my ambition as well.' Georgia was defensive.

'But you have an opening here, in the dairy. I'm sure there are lots of things you could do for us.'

'Like office work? No, thank you. I want something much more connected with what I'm doing at Uni. There must be someone who'll want us, don't you think, Giles?'

'Definitely. I'd also like to travel a bit

before I'm tied to a job. Not sure how or when or where to go, though.'

'Me too. We talked about going to Paris, didn't we?'

'Maybe. I'm thinking more of the South of France. Van Gogh country and all the Provençal artists.'

'Yes, of course. Maybe we could go grape-picking to pay for it.'

'Grapes are never ready to be picked in July. You can forget that one.' Her father spoke rather adamantly. 'Ridiculous idea. No, you need to think about working properly. Get yourself a proper job and earn some money.'

Fortunately, Nicola came into the room at that point, cutting off Georgia's retaliation.

'Lunch will be ready in a few minutes. Can I have a sherry, dear?' George poured one and handed it to her. 'Thank you. Did Daddy say I've got myself a job?'

'No! At the charity shop?'

'Yes indeed. Two mornings a week. I went on Friday and thoroughly enjoyed

247

it. It wasn't a bit like a jumble sale. They only have fairly good stuff, and it's all hanging on rails.'

'Excellent. I'm delighted to hear it; I said you'd like it.'

'No more endlessly boring days wondering what to do with myself. I'll go and dish up the vegetables now.'

'And how is the dairy?'

'Pretty good there too. We've bought a couple of new farms and so production is better. We're hoping to expand into a new area soon.'

'Good. All sounds positive. And the Aunts? Still causing you grief?'

'Well, yes, they are. Can't seem to get anything done without another board meeting. But, we'll cope. We have done so far.'

'It all sounds a rather safe company, from what Georgia has told me,' Giles said.

'Well, I suppose it is. It's very much a family firm and, well, I'd hoped my daughters would both be a part of it. Seems I'm to be unlucky.'

'Oh Daddy, you know I never wanted to be a part of it. It shouldn't be a surprise to you. And Maria is much too clever to want to be there. I think you'll have to make do with your nephews. They're enjoying it all, aren't they?'

'I suppose so. Come on. Let's have lunch.'

It was a typical Sunday lunch for the Wilkins family. For Giles, it was a relatively new experience: the formality of them all sitting round the table and making polite conversation seemed somewhat alien to him. But he sat it out and dutifully answered the questions fired at him. Until Nicola fired a question that somewhat floored him.

'So, Giles, do you intend to marry my daughter?' He gasped and looked at Georgia. She looked uncomfortable and wriggled in her seat. 'Well?'

'I don't know. We haven't discussed it.'

'It seems to me perhaps you should have. I don't know what your living premises are like, but to have the pair of you under one roof . . . well, *really*.'

'Mummy, I *told* you, I have my own room. It's all perfectly decent.'

'Well, I don't like it. Are you serious about each other?'

Georgia stared at Giles, not knowing what to say. He drew himself up and spoke clearly.

'Perhaps one day, before too long, we shall get engaged. We love each other very much and don't intend to spoil that. I assure I shall come and see you both before we do get engaged. I want to have a job by then in any case.'

'Well said, my boy,' said George. 'I don't want her getting wed while you're still at college. Stay away from her till after that.'

'I think we should leave now,' said Georgia, still smarting from her mother's questioning.

'But you haven't had coffee yet.' Nicola was suddenly embarrassed and realised she had possibly made a fool of herself. 'Please don't go yet. Have some coffee first.'

The couple looked at each other

questioningly. Giles nodded, and so Georgia agreed. Her mother went into the kitchen to make it, while her father moved some of the empty dishes and took them out. Georgia smiled.

'Now, there's a first. I've never seen him clear the table before in his life.'

'You two lovebirds stay there. I'll take the rest out.' Maria picked up several plates and took them out.

'I'm so sorry, Giles. That was so embarrassing.'

'Don't worry. It's quite an idea, though, isn't it?'

'What is?'

'For us to get engaged.'

'Really?'

'Would you consider it?'

'Of course I would. Oh, Giles, thank you for asking me. Let's get engaged.'

'Shall I ask your father's permission today?'

'No. Let's leave it for a while. Let's just be engaged and only we know it. We can't get married for ages anyway.'

'Oh, I don't know. We could do very

251

easily. We can go on living with Mum and be married, instead of trying to find somewhere else to live. She'd be delighted. She's very fond of you.'

'But you told Daddy you wanted to find work first.'

'I know I did. But it occurred to me, if we were married as soon as we finish college, we could go abroad for our honeymoon. It may not be a conventional sort of honeymoon, but would that matter?'

'Not to me, it wouldn't. Oh Giles, how wonderful.' She leaned over and kissed him. They were still kissing when Maria came back.

'Oh, go somewhere else, can't you?'

'Sorry, little sister. We're in love. You just wait till you are. It's a lovely feeling.'

THE END

Books by Chrissie Loveday
in the Linford Romance Library:

HER HEART'S DESIRE
FROM THIS DAY ON
WHERE THE HEART IS
OUT OF THE BLUE
TOMORROW'S DREAMS
DARE TO LOVE
WHERE LOVE BELONGS
TO LOVE AGAIN
DESTINY CALLING
THE SURGEON'S MISTAKE
GETTING A LIFE
ONWARD AND UPWARD

We do hope that you have enjoyed reading this large print book.

Did you know that all of our titles are available for purchase?

We publish a wide range of high quality large print books including:
Romances, Mysteries, Classics
General Fiction
Non Fiction and Westerns

Special interest titles available in large print are:
The Little Oxford Dictionary
Music Book, Song Book
Hymn Book, Service Book

Also available from us courtesy of Oxford University Press:
Young Readers' Dictionary
(large print edition)
Young Readers' Thesaurus
(large print edition)

For further information or a free brochure, please contact us at:
Ulverscroft Large Print Books Ltd.,
The Green, Bradgate Road, Anstey,
Leicester, LE7 7FU, England.
Tel: (00 44) 0116 236 4325
Fax: (00 44) 0116 234 0205

THE SECRET OF THE SILVER LOCKET

Jill Barry

Orphan Grace Walker will come of age in 1925, having spent years as companion to the daughter of an aristocratic family. Grace believes her origins are humble, but as her birthday approaches, an encounter with young American professor Harry Gresham offers the chance of love and a new life. What could possibly prevent her from seizing happiness? A silver locket holds a vital clue, and a letter left by Grace's late mother reveals shocking news. Only Harry can piece the puzzle together . . .

THE AWAKENING HEART

Jean M. Long

When Tamsin's uncle and aunt take a holiday, leaving the family business — Lambourne Catering — in the charge of the younger generation, everyone must pitch in. Working at a near-disastrous dinner party, Tamsin meets Fraser, whose initially abrasive attitude hides a warm and understanding man beneath. Despite herself, Tamsin feels a growing attraction to him. But Rob, the man who broke her heart years ago, has returned — and seems to be carrying a torch for her once more . . .